RICOCHET

SASCHA MASETTO

────────────────

RICOCHET

────────────────

CHAPTER

1

June, 2019

Capron, Illinois was the tiniest of suburban towns, overshadowed by the towering metropolis of Chicago. Nothing notable had ever come out of Capron, which didn't bother its residents. Most people knew each other, and if they didn't, there was only one degree of separation. There were two bars in the entire town, so on any given night you were bound to run into a friend, or in some cases, an enemy. In one of these dingy watering holes José stood at the counter, staring down at his watered-down gin and tonic. Tiny bubbles rose up, slid between the ice, then bounced around the surface for a split second before vanishing.

José was lanky, yet athletic. He was that kind of teenager who could splurge daily yet never gain a pound. His curly dark hair fell over his angular face so often he carried around a hairband, but mostly he would just swing it around his index finger. After nineteen years, he had never cared much for fashion or appearances, which never tarnished him in the eyes of others. His ne'er-do-well attitude made him seem attractively unflappable. This, like for most teenagers, was only a façade.

"Asshole! Get over here!" yelled Gary. José grabbed his drink and turned to a booth where Gary, Phil, and Bernie, José's pimply, but loyal friends sucked on beers and Juul pens. Gary, a plump, freckled tyke shoved Phil, an already-balding, muscled country bumpkin farther into the booth to make room for José.

Bernie, a half Korean, half Canadian kid whose puberty was hitting like a boxer, raised his glass, and the other three followed suit. "Happy nine-" Gary slugged Bernie in the shoulder. The tattooed bartender glanced up and rolled his eyes. He needed the business dearly.

Bernie and José had met in preschool and had been inseparable ever since. Gary had moved into town for his parents' work, befriended Phil, and then all four were randomly assigned together for a school project in middle school. They were given three weeks to make a poster board about the local Native American tribes, so as per tradition, they spent two and half weeks blowing it off, discovering a shared love for marijuana stolen from Phil's older brother. They had gotten a C minus.

"I appreciate it," José chuckled, "even if my twenty third birthday is in two months." All four glanced up at the bartender who was busy serving a pair of heavy truckers.

"Shit, it's her." muttered Bernie. The four swung their heads in unison to the entrance where Sarah, a small brunette with eyes too big for her face and a recently abandoned goth phase, stood with five of her best friends. They whispered to each other conspiratorially, peeking back at the boys. Gary, Phil, and Bernie peered cautiously at José, who took a sudden interest in the grain of the table.

"I knew we shouldn't have come here." Phil murmured. José shook his head, "Really, she's nothing anymore." He downed his drink.

"Another round?" José stumbled over to the bar, brandishing a credit card. His friends made no moves to stop him, especially after the stress of entering the establishment incognito.

Later at some nocturnal hour, José, beyond plastered, pushed his way into a large airplane hangar, peppered with several small prop planes. "Oye, papá!" José smacked the metal wall. José careened toward the closest two-seater prop plane, opened the door, and climbed in. The door swung shut behind him.

Angel, José's paunchy, stern, Puerto Rican father, dressed in boxers and a ratty wife-beater, stepped inside the hangar, rubbing his eyes. Seeing nothing, Angel threw his arms up and left, muttering under his breath. It wasn't rare to hear José rattling around at all hours of the night, plus, it was the boy's birthday. But tomorrow wasn't, so Angel rubbed his hands in anticipation, contemplating which cruel manner he would wake up his dehydrated offspring in the morning.

✛

Sunlight filtered into the hangar. Inside the storage area of the tail of the prop plane, José slept, tranquilized by a liver full of cheap gin. He had spread the plane's emergency blanket over his curled-up body, giving the appearance of a covered pile of equipment.

A busted pick-up wheezed into the hangar, honking once. A woman jumped down, looking around at the planes. She was small but sturdy, with a short straight haircut and dark skin. Dressed in a tight jumpsuit, one could see that she avidly exercised, with more weights than cardio. To combat the fear of making new friends, Diane put all her focus on her studies and hobbies, ignoring any opportunities for social interaction. Her Pakistani parents had given up on trying to connect with her. Diane was a physicist, tenured at Northwestern, but had quit due to a lack of patience and respect for academia.

Angel, now shaved and donning grey overalls, approached. "Ms. Kohli?" he asked with an out-stretched hand. Bits of toilet paper hung off his chin.

"Thank you, I know it's early," Diane responded quickly, shaking his hand, "All good to go?"

Angel nodded, "Of course." He gestured to the nearest plane.

"Great." Diane pulled the passenger door open, extracted a large black duffle bag, and handed it to Angel. "Here you go."

"Where do you want this?"

"Oh no, that's your payment."

Angel peeked inside and felt his heart skip. He had never seen that many bills in one place. He sputtered, "Umm, this is...way more than we had talked about..."

"This reservation was so far in advance and I really appreciate the manner of privacy which you've dealt with this whole thing."

"I could buy a new plane with this," admitted Angel. Diane shrugged and skipped to the back of the truck. She opened the bed and pointed to several large metal boxes, each the size of a coffin and covered in solar panels. "All this goes on the plane."

"Perfect, I'll load them up after the inspection."

Diane shook her head vigorously, glancing anxiously out of the hangar, "Don't worry about that, just make sure there's a full tank."

Angel shrugged, not about to argue with such a generous benefactor.

Ten minutes later, he waved to Diane who taxied the plane out toward the runway. Diane had contacted him a month ago and had offered exorbitant amounts of cash to rent a plane, continuously hinting that he should not keep any record of their transactions or communications. He was glad that her ludicrous offers had actually come to fruition. Finally, he could afford a new plane and a trip back to Puerto Rico with José this winter to visit his grandmother. Angel slouched back into the hangar.

"José! ¿Dónde estás?"

In the plane, Diane took out a small metallic case, roughly the size of a smartphone, from her backpack. She pressed the top side of the box which slid down, revealing a small LED touch screen displaying these symbols 'J10(31)'.

Diane carefully placed the box into her jumpsuit's breast pocket. She accelerated the tiny craft into the sky.

Once in the air, Diane took in the tens of thousands of feet between her and the ground. Below her in the distance lay Chicago and the surrounding metropolis. Willis Tower shot up like a beacon. Its black sides contrasted starkly with the ivory antennae that extended up from its roof. Diane remembered visiting it, taking the elevator all the way up to the viewing floor where tourists sat in protruding glass boxes overlooking the city. Upon stepping into one of these, she had felt nothing but disgust for civilization. The grime and pestilence had made her want to vomit.

José began to stir. His hangover had just reached the stage where hunger became more important than his throbbing head. Fantasies of greasy omelets and orange juice floated into his mind. The teenager stirred, realizing that his makeshift bed rocking violently wasn't a dream.

Diane pulled the yoke and the plane soared up. In the back, José slid off onto the floor, utterly discombobulated. Diane made sure to turn off all radio communications with the ground. Once their altitude leveled off to a lofty twenty-eight thousand feet, Diane pulled out the device from her breast pocket. A large green button appeared on the touchscreen. Diane tapped without hesitation. The screen turned black, then a few lines of text appeared in its place: *'Transportation Sequence Activated - Est. Chronological Transference: 338'*

Taking a deep breath, Diane pushed the wheel. The plane tilted into a steep nosedive, just as José jumped to his feet and practically fell into the cockpit.

"What the fuck are you doing?!" Diane screamed, scared shitless of the unexpected, half naked intruder. The plane lurched forward and gained speed as it began to freefall. José pitched forward, catching himself in the doorway. The device slipped out of Diane's hand onto the control deck.

'Commencing Transference'

Diane unsuccessfully tried to unbuckle her seatbelt for one final attempt at reaching the device. The ground rushed up towards them. José closed his eyes. Her fingers grazed the device, just as a ball of blue glowing energy materialized from the gadget, expanding quickly.

The glimmering sphere surrounded the plane, changed from blue to green, and vanished, taking the plane and all of its contents along. A rush of air hit the ground, causing the trees to rustle violently, and then silence.

José clenched his eyes shut.

"You okay?" came a voice.

José unclenched his eyes, but little light came to him. He wondered if he had actually opened his eyes. Then, they adjusted, and grew wide.

Diane was preparing the plane for descent. They cruised at a level altitude. The sky was dark, stars glittered in the sky and the moon hung ahead to the left, taunting him.

"What happened?" was all that José managed.

"What were you doing back there?"

"Is there an eclipse going on or something?" José rubbed his eyes, moving towards a porthole, seeing nothing but trees lit by moonlight. "Am I dead?"

"You really shouldn't have been back there."

José squinted, "Where are we?"

Diane bit her lip, "Guess I should have let him do an inspection."

"What happened? How is it suddenly so dark?"

Diane pressed a few controls, lowering the landing gear. "Let me land first, I'll explain."

José studied the pitch-black ground, "Must be a countywide outage."

Diane flew a few more miles, as she was only able to see the ground by moonlight and needed to find a clear runway. She and José argued about where to land, until finally they decided on a long open field surrounded by sparse oak trees. They circled several times, unable to agree at which angle to direct the plane down.

After a bumpy landing José flung open the door and hopped out, pulling out his phone. No service. After turning on and off airplane mode, José frowned and restarted it. Diane jumped down next to him, scanning the surroundings. The tall oak trees swayed all around them like wispy giants. The sound of millions of cicadas uninterrupted sent chills down her spine.

José asked, "Can you get any bars?" Diane extracted the metal box from her pocket, opening the screen and checking it.

"What's your name?" Diane asked.

"José. Could I borrow that to call my dad?"

Diane bounced on her feet, "Well, José, I'm not really sure how to tell you this, but..."

"But...?"

"We're still in Illinois. It's just that..."

José crossed his arms.

"We're in the year 1681. Once this device reaches a certain acceleration, it transports everything in a 13-meter radius into the past. That's why I had to nose dive. To reach the proper acceleration."

José began to laugh, "88 miles per hour, Marty?"

From the darkness, a projectile whizzed into José, throwing him backwards. He screamed. It took a second for Diane to realize what had happened. At first, she thought that he had tripped, but upon seeing the large arrow protrude gruesomely out of José's shoulder, Diane dropped, hyperventilating. Blood gushed from his shoulder, as he writhed on the ground. Diane crawled over to him, cupping his mouth. Adrenaline kicked in, and she suddenly felt more in control than she had in a long time.

"Shut up. SHUT UP. If you want to survive, do what I say. We're gonna get back on the plane and fly off, okay? On the count of five, I'm gonna help you up, okay? Got it!?"

José nodded weakly, so Diane slid her arm underneath José's shivering torso. "On five, okay? One, two, three, four, five-"

Diane used all her strength to pull up José. Once on their feet, they froze. Surrounding them in a tight semi-circle, stood six Native American warriors.

June, 1681

The six Sauk warriors were as still and as quiet as stat-
ues, their arrows notched and aimed at Diane with stoic
composure. She knew the wrong move would result in six
arrows stuck in her head. The warriors gazed at the airplane, while keeping their aim on Diane. The roaring metal
beast that flew faster than any bird was the only reason
they kept their distance.

Chaska, a broad-shouldered warrior, lowered his bow
and took a step towards the duo. He had a multitude of
scars and tattoos running up and down his face and torso.
His jet-black hair was pulled back into a ponytail. He wore
just a simple loincloth with sandals. Slowly, he began conversing with his comrades in the Sauk tongue.

Mahka, a similarly dressed, wiry, hawk-eyed warrior, adjusted his bow to aim at Diane's chest, growling something in response.

As José lost more and more blood, he began to slip into unconsciousness. Diane felt his deadweight lean onto her and tried to shake him awake, whispering his name. This caused the warriors to pull their bows tighter. Diane grunted, using all her strength to hold up José.

Chaska stopped a few paces away and drew a long knife from his belt. He motioned to Diane to let go of José. Diane lowered the bleeding teenager to the ground.

"Please," Diane said in Sauk. Chaska and the others jumped at hearing her speak their native tongue. Chaska asked her slowly to explain herself. Diane strained herself, trying to translate the right words in her head. Glacially, she raised her arms and carefully pronounced, "We do not come to hurt. We come to help."

Chaska took a step forward, "You speak our language? How?"

"I have eaten...no...I have studied it for a long horse- a long time!"

"What is that beast behind you?"

Diane shook her head, not understanding. Chaska wagged his blade at the airplane, raising one eyebrow.

"That is no beast. It is a..." Diane trailed off, realizing there was no word for machine or airplane in the Sauk language. She had spent years learning Sauk, tracking down the few remaining native speakers, yet even still, the version she was familiar with had had at least three centuries to evolve. At the very minimum, she knew how the grammar worked and some elementary vocabulary. "It is a...creation."

The warriors glanced at each other suspiciously. Chaska noticed the fear and exhaustion in her eyes and lowered his knife. The others did not drop their aim.

"Let us kill her and take it," grunted Mahka.

"Do not kill me! I come to help!" cried Diane. Mahka pulled back on his bow, "She is lying." Chaska waved down Mahka, who reluctantly lowered his bow.

"What do you mean 'help'? How could you possibly help us?"

Diane took a deep breath, calculating her response. She wasn't going to tell the whole truth, but she didn't want to lie, "I am from a distant world. In my world, we know much. So much that I must share my knowledge with you."

"Tell me," asked Chaska. Diane looked down at José, who was now completely unconscious. She pleaded, "If somebody doesn't help my friend, he will die. I will tell you all that I know but you must help him first."

Chaska looked down at the boy. His clothes were like those of the woman, completely alien. Mahka appeared at Chaska's side and pulled him to the side.

After a few seconds of bickering, Chaska put his foot down. He asked Diane gruffly, "Can your creation move on the ground?"

Once inside, Chaska stared at the interior of the plane, entranced by the plethora of shiny objects whose purposes escaped him. Diane nervously glanced at him from behind the yoke. They were taxiing along the bumpy terrain as Mahka and three of the warriors rode on horseback next to the plane. The final warrior tended to José's shoulder wound in the back of the plane.

"Where are you from?" Chaska asked Diane, who rubbed her neck, uncomfortable.

"My home is very far away. Its name would mean nothing to you," she decided to not clarify which measurement of distance she was using.

"Do they speak our language there?"

Diane shook her head.

Chaska tilted his head, "In your land, does everybody ride in these creations?"

"Sometimes. Only for great distances."

"Is he from your land?" Chaska gestured to José.

"He's a neighbor."

Chaska wanted to ask more questions, but they were nearing the Sauk village, about a hundred white and brown Teepees marked by rising smoke.

The first rays of dawn crested from the east, illuminating the already bustling tribe. Diane craned to get a better look, her nose squished against the front windshield. Men and women mingled together, trading materials and gossip, while the children played with sticks and small dogs. Everyone was either dressed in buckskin or nothing at all. All action ceased at the sight and sound of the approaching caravan of horseback riders and prop plane. Chaska instructed Diane to stop near the edge of the vast encampment. Chaska had used the word which Diane understood as "village", but she thought it more appropriate to be called a "town". The tribespeople gathered and watched intently from a distance, subdued only slightly by the familiar warriors who surrounded their metal prize.

Diane glanced back at José. He looked deathly pale, but his chest still moved up and down. The warrior who had just finished patching up José's wound gave Diane a smirk and leapt down from the plane. Chaska rose, pulling Diane up with him.

"He will survive. He just needs to rest."

Chaska yanked Diane off the plane, just quickly enough that Diane stumbled. Murmurs ran through the crowd as they jostled for a better view. Chaska began to speak loudly and at such a pace that Diane couldn't translate in time, "We were patrolling the western border when we heard a great noise from above. We tracked it and took the invaders hostage. This woman is from a distant land, where they fly in metal beasts."

The tribe fell completely silent. Chaska continued, "She made no attempt to attack our men, and she even claims to want to help us, that she has great knowledge. Until the elders have made a decision, she is our prisoner." He clearly enunciated the last sentence so Diane could understand.

Diane felt the tribespeople's apprehension, burning into her with distrustful fear. Chaska faced Diane but continued to talk loudly so the entire tribe could hear, "As our prisoner, I demand you show us your power."

Diane sputtered, "What?"

"Give us an example of your great knowledge."

"Hmm..." said Diane, "It's difficult to roast- PROVE my ability. I can tell you many things about the future but they will happen in chicken moons."

The villagers laughed. Chaska suppressed a smile. Diane looked around at the villagers, embarrassed. Chaska raised his hand and the tribe fell silent. "Tell us."

Diane took a deep breath, then said, "White people will invade this land, as they already have in the east. More and more will come from across the great sea. They will murder you. You will fight, but they will win. Eventually, they will rule this land from end to end."

The tribe remained silent. Some had witnessed the violent predatory nature of the Europeans and the rest had heard plenty of stories. Chaska countered, "This is our land, we know it better than them. How can they possibly win?"

"They have better weapons."

Chaska thought, then said, "Every day, we get more and more guns"

Diane shook her head, "They also use weapons that you cannot purchase. They bring diseases from their world, for which you will have no apple- CURE! You will have no cure."

Onawa, an old woman, who had just as many wrinkles as wits, revered as the wisest in the tribe, stepped towards the newcomer, "I have seen the cruelty and ruthlessness of their race. You claimed to want to help us..."

Diane opened her mouth, but before she could respond, a groan from the plane pulled her and everybody's attention. José stood in the doorway, staring dumbfoundedly at Diane and the tribe. "What in the actual fuck?"

Inside the plane, for the next hour, José and Diane argued while the tribe waited outside, all straining to hear their conversation even though none knew English.

"Take me home!" pleaded José, as he dropped all pretense of modesty and fell to his knees, "This is not funny anymore, please! I'll do anything, just take me back!"

"I don't really know what to tell you. I can't."

José slammed his fist into the side of the plane's interior, jumping to his feet "Give me the goddamned keys and I'll fly myself home!"

"*Home* won't exist for at least a few hundred years."

He demanded, with clenched fists, "Do you expect me to believe you?"

An idea came to Diane. She grinned and said, "I'll prove it to you. First, I gotta talk to them before they decide to kill us." José grabbed an oatmeal bar from a cabinet and stalked into the cockpit. He threw himself angrily down in the pilot's seat and peered out at the crowd, some of whom had gone back to their morning obligations. Most stood in a large semi-circle, conversing about the metal beast. Diane yelled, "Chaska!"

Chaska appeared at the plane doorway, eyebrow cocked. In his language, Diane pointed to one of the large boxes on the plane and asked him, "Help me carry this."

Chaska shook his head. Diane sputtered, "What do you mean?"

"I'm not your servant and you're not my guest."

Diane rolled her eyes, reminding herself that, by traveling back in time, overt, childish masculinity was going to be much more obnoxious. "Would it make you feel better if two of your men carried it out? You can act like it's loot." Chaska waved at two men to approach, "I'll act like it's loot, because it is loot."

The large metal box was hefted towards the center of the crowd which buzzed around in anticipation. As they placed it on the dirt, the tribe gathered in closer. Chaska and Diane pushed through the tightening crowd, and Diane noticed that the tribespeople gave her a wide berth, as if she might be carrying one of the diseases that she had mentioned. Once at the box, Diane typed on a keypad, and the box's latch popped open. Chaska was too interested in its contents to remember to demand permission, so Diane proceeded to lift open the top. She extracted a small glass vial, turned to Onawa, and handed it to the wise woman. "Now you have a cure to one of the diseases that the white ones will bring," Diane announced dramatically. Onawa held up the vial to the sun, swishing around the clear liquid. Diane leaned back into the box, pulling a protective covering off an intricate machine. The entire tribe peered inside, unsure of what they were looking at.

"What are we looking at?" asked Onawa.

Diane enunciated in English, "A direct metal laser sintering 3d printer." This gibberish, of course, was met with blank stares. Diane switched back to their language, "With this, you'll be able to create as many weapons and tools as you want."

-

June, 1681

Diane and José soared in the plane above what could only be Lake Michigan, just without the conglomeration of skyscrapers and houses lining its shores. A luscious green carpet covered the area where José believed Millennium Park and its famous reflective bean should be. From their lofty perch, not a single building came into view. Diane could feel his infuriated glaze bore into the back of her head.

"Who are you?" José demanded, "some escaped mental patient?"

Diane gave him a look of frustration. José decided to play along to see if he could extract some information on their exact whereabouts, "So you invented time travel?"

She didn't answer and stared forward.

"Are you from the future?"

Diane exhaled, "Of course, so are you."

"No, I mean the future of my time?"

"Yes, your time was my past."

"And you can't bring me back to 2019 because it will no longer exist?"

Diane nodded, "Exactly. I'm very sorry..."

"That thing you gave them?" José was referring to the advanced 3D metal sintering printer that Diane had gifted to the Sauk tribe. It was capable of making extremely small, intricate mechanical parts from raw materials. Diane nodded, "It's all part of a plan. One plan of many." Diane gestured to the back of the plane where the remaining large metal boxes rattled.

José fumed, "Sure."

"I didn't ask for you to be sleeping in the back of the plane I rented!"

"The plane you stole from my dad! You weren't going to return it!"

"Look, we gotta make best with what we got."

"He's gonna freak," José said, holding his head in his hands. Diane gulped. The distraught teenager slumped down in his seat, thinking hard.

"So, what exactly are you trying to do here?"

Diane cleared her throat, "We landed in 1681, which predates major European colonialism of the American continents. The only way to curb this is to help the native population defend their rightfully owned land. With the proper resources and direction, the Europeans will see their mission as pointless, retreat to the eastern hemisphere and respect the Native Americans' dominion and set up trade. Instead of genocide, cohabitation."

"Great," José muttered, "Fantastic plan."

Diane began to prepare the plane for descent.

"Why wouldn't you travel back to before Europeans arrived?"

"It's too far in the past. I couldn't think of a way to reach the proper acceleration. The transference device requires more acceleration to travel farther."

Chaska, Onawa, and a few other elders gathered around as Diane and José stepped down from the plane. Onawa bowed her head to Diane, "We need you to explain how it works."

"What is she saying?" José asked Diane.

"They want to know what to use the 3d printer for."

José deflated and stomped back into the plane.

Diane gave her attention to Onawa, stepping down off the plane, "Forget the 3d printer for now. First let's concentrate on something that others already have."

Inside the plane, José paced back and forth. His mind raced furiously. Obviously, he couldn't stay here. His eyes fell upon the ignition of the plane. Diane kept the key inside her breast pocket at all times, but José had grown up with the plane so finding a spare took no time at all. Once he secured it in his pocket, he peeked out the window. The tribe elders huddled around Diane who was describing something in great detail, waving her hands in the air while her spectators grew more and more puzzled.

"You'll have to trust me," Diane explained to the elders, "I wouldn't be able to explain to you many things in your language because you don't have words for them. You will have to invent new words for these things, and then pass them on."

Diane rushed over to one of the large metal boxes, typed in the code on the keypad, and pulled out a binder full of papers, all covered in obscure symbols. It was an alphabet, one which she had created to provide a complete orthography based on the Sauk language. She passed them out to the elders. "Your people must develop a written language."

Chaska spat, "This will not help us fight. The strength of a warrior comes from his heart, not his words."

"The strength of a warrior comes from the words of his bees-COMRADES, not bees. Once you learn how to write and read, you'll be able to send messages across long distances, using-"

Chaska countered, "We use smoke to communicate."

"Smoke signals can communicate if somebody is coming, if there are many and if they are dangerous, nothing more. Imagine you could tell a fellow tribesman how many warriors there are exactly, how many are armed, how many horses they have, how many guns they hold, which direction they are headed, how young they are, how fast they're going, and what they look like. Plus, as long as you have a receiving device near you, you won't even need to see the smoke. You could be anywhere."

Chaska and the elders fell silent. Diane held up a sheet of paper, "All you have to do is learn this. Then the world can be yours."

José stumbled off the plane, almost tripping on the last step. His hair was disheveled, he'd been stress scratching. He grumbled, "Let's talk. I'm sorry, okay?" Diane nodded and the elders began reviewing the stacks of papers. She walked over to the exhausted teenager, laying a steady hand on his shoulder.

"I've thought about it and I want to help you," José said, "what can I do?"

"For now, nothing, just sit back and relax. Get an early night."

José nodded, doing everything in his power not to explode with rage. He jumped back into the plane, Diane watching him suspiciously.

Inside the cockpit, José peered out the window, making sure Diane was still outside before using the spare key to open a compartment in the lower left wall of the cockpit. He pulled out a small pistol and slipped it into his jeans' waistband.

June, 1681

Diane watched the sun rising above the plains. The crisp, untouched landscape glowed. Red mulberries, black-gum, cottonwood, and white oak trees, of all shapes and sizes dominated the backdrop, contrasting starkly with the white and brown teepees and grey smoke that lay before the ex-physicist. Even though she hadn't slept a wink, Diane felt more energized than ever before. She held the ability to change everything. José was a factor, but she felt confident that she would be able to subdue his effect on history.

Diane glanced around at Sauk camp, which appeared to be oddly deserted. Chaska, who was painted head to toe in several earthy colors, approached holding a few sheets of paper with their newly written language.

"Why are you doing this?" he asked.

Diane smiled, "to save you all."

Chaska shook his head and asked, "Why are *you* specifically doing this? Why haven't your people visited us before?"

"Nobody knew how."

Chaska nodded curtly, then raised his chin, "I want to show you something. Is the boy with you?"

"José!" called Diane. José stepped down from the plane, pretending to stretch from a good night's sleep. He also hadn't slept a wink.

"Are we taking off yet?"

Diane shook her head, then motioned him to join them. Chaska had already about-faced and was speeding through the camp. Diane and José jogged to catch up.

The two foreigners slowed to halt at the edge of the teepees. In front of them lay a large open grass field, slightly larger than a soccer pitch. Hundreds of men, all painted like Chaska, swarmed around the field, each one carrying a large stick with a leather pouch hanging off one end. There were several large water-filled barrels spread around the field. One after the other, the men would run over to the barrel, dip their stick into the water, and then prance over to a group of ornately dressed Shamans who waved their hands around each freshly dipped stick.

Occasionally, a stick-holder would display his arm to a Shaman, who would take a tiny blade and nick the man on the arm. After at least a quarter of an hour, a cry broke out amongst the crowd. The stick-holders formed a large circle, linking arms. They began to chant, dance, and shake their sticks back and forth.

Onawa appeared behind the pair. "This is *Little War*," instructed Onawa, and pointed to two large wooden poles on either side of the field, "Those totems are the objectives."

The circle broke apart and two teams formed on either side, surrounding each totem. Diane and José couldn't guess how the two teams were formed, as there were no determinable differences marking each side. A Shaman, carrying a round rock the size of grapefruit, slowly walked to the center of the field. He placed the rock on the ground, blessed it with a few incantations, and quickly departed. The tribe fell quiet, leaving only sounds of the birds and rustlings of the trees.

A series of cries went up on each side, and both rushed towards the rock in the middle. Most just attacked others with their sticks, whacking and blocking, wielding them as swords. The rock was lost from sight until it was flung above the men's heads, landing with a sickening crunch on the head of a young boy, who crumpled to the ground. Instead of helping him, the mob crowded around him, fighting violently for the rock. José spun on his heels and fled back towards the plane. Diane smiled apologetically to Onawa and ran after him.

An hour later, Diane steered the plane while José tried to come to terms with what they had just witnessed. They hadn't spoken more than a couple words since boarding. Chaska squatted behind them, gripping the sides of the cockpit with his eyes closed, muttering and shaking. He was bruised and exhausted from the 'Little War' but mostly motion-sick from his first ever flight. José wished Chaska hadn't demanded to come.

Diane joked in English, "Should've guessed he wouldn't be so hot here."

José blinked dazedly, "Where exactly are we going?"

"We're looking for clay deposits to make bricks," Diane craned to inspect a hillside, "We'll use the bricks to make furnaces which lets them make steel products." Before José could protest, Diane had begun the descent.

Chaska vaulted out of the parked plane, kissing the ground with a fiery passion. Diane pointed to a squat hill bordered by a lazy river, no more than a few dozen yards wide. Brownish grey boulders peeked out from the other side of the creek. "Bingo."

The click of a pistol cock made Diane freeze.

"On your knees. Tell him to do the same." Diane could sense José's pistol muzzle inches from her head.

Chaska glanced up to see José pointing a strange metal object at Diane's head. Even though he'd never seen something like it before, the look on Diane's face told him everything. He took a step towards José who swung the pistol toward him. "Back up, motherfucker! Diane, tell him to get on his knees!"

Diane quickly conferred to Chaska the significance of the mechanism, who reluctantly knelt beside her.

"I'm taking the plane. I will be back, but I need to see something for myself."

"You have no idea what's out there!"

José scoffed, "Just stay here, I'll be back to pick you up."

Diane trembled in rage, "No! This wasn't ..."

Without warning, Chaska lunged at José who fired. The bullet ripped through Chaska's lower abdomen. Diane screamed as Chaska flopped to the ground.

"Oh fuck..." José gasped, "I didn't..."

Diane scrambled to Chaska's side, pressing on his wound, trying to stop the bleeding. José began to shake, still pointing the pistol at Chaska who convulsed unnaturally.

"Gauze and wraps! On the plane!" Diane yelled at José, "Please, for the love of god!" José stood, paralyzed for a full ten seconds before finally breaking from his trance and stumbling into the plane. He returned with the first aid kit. Diane began working to clean and cover the wound. The bullet had ripped cleanly through and Chaska was still breathing, albeit weakly. José backed up and clambered into the plane. Diane was so focused on bandaging Chaska that she hardly noticed the plane's engine turn over.

"José!"

Tears streaming down his face, José gunned the plane forward, lifting off. Diane leapt to her feet, screeching expletives.

Hours later, Diane knelt beside Chaska's punctured torso. Underneath a pile of gauze and tape, the bleeding had subsided and from his labored breathing, Diane figured the bullet hadn't pierced a major organ, but he wasn't going to escape infection. Diane silently prayed that José would return to his senses. She had been scanning the skyline for hours.

The sun had begun to set and darkness crept over the land. Diane took off her jacket and swaddled Chaska with it. She stiffly pushed herself to her feet, "We need water, I'll be right back."

Diane took three steps and stopped, straining to see into the surrounding bushes, all obscured by long shadows. Cautiously, Diane took a few more steps. A twig snapped behind her. She swung around to see a giant feral cougar inching towards the supine man. Its mouth hung open, giant fangs glistening with saliva.

José sobbed and sobbed. He flew steadily east. There was no law enforcement, no justice system, and definitely no disappointed Puerto Rican father. Now, there was only him, a small two-seater prop plane that was quickly running out of gas, a pistol with a few more shots, and a metal device that was either a gimmick or actually held the secrets to time travel. He needed proof. Perhaps the lake he had seen flying with Diane wasn't Lake Michigan. He was going to scour eastwards until he found evidence.

June, 1681

The cougar took a step forward, tail flicking back and forth. Diane trembled, her vision wavered and blurred. She had no experience with vicious wild animals. *What should I do? Is this a cougar or a mountain lion? Are those different things? What the fuck do I do?!*

The large feline crept closer, now only a few feet away from Chaska, licking its lips at the sight and smell of his blood. Diane stepped over Chaska, putting herself between the beast and its meal. She yelled and waved her arms wildly. The cougar hesitated for a split second, then pounced on Diane, who screamed and tumbled backwards, tripping over Chaska.

Large hindquarter claws, each inches long and razor sharp, dug into Diane's thighs. She furiously grabbed the cougar's neck, trying to strangle it as its front claws battered her arms. The mountain cat drew more and more blood from Diane, her grip on its neck began to loosen.

Suddenly, the cougar fell limp, sprawling on top of Diane, its hindquarters still lodged in her legs. Chaska fell to the ground, and seconds later was unconscious. He had buried a knife into the cougar's head. Whimpering, Diane pushed the feline corpse off and inspected her wounds. The gashes in her thighs were tremendously deep. She couldn't move her legs. She could still control her arms but even the slightest movement upwards caused her nerves to explode in pain. Unwilling to raise her arms high enough to check her face, she licked around her mouth and found no blood.

She fell back onto the ground, crying and hyperventilating. Adrenaline kept her awake even though she was more exhausted than she had ever been. *How are we going to survive the night? How are we going to get back to the camp?*

Diane huddled close to Chaska, trying to share her body warmth. She nudged his face with her chin. He needed to stay awake. A rustle behind them made Diane's heart sink. Just the thing they needed, another cougar. Diane craned her neck up and saw five human figures approaching.

"Oh, thank god."

José had been flying, talking to himself, and crying, but just as he spotted the moon reflecting off the Atlantic Ocean, he ran out of tears and things to say. He also ran out of gas. He directed his descent towards an oblong island that he knew by only one name: Long Island.

A moment before José's wheels bounced on the ground, the fuel gauge hit zero. José taxied the plane to a stop in the middle of a dirt road, lined by tall grass and sparse maple trees. Clouds moved in.

José slumped over the steering wheel, overwhelmed by the events of the last two days. He was sure that he made it to a coast. He had parked closely enough to walk to the water where he could test if it was salt or fresh water and then hopefully find somebody to help him get back to Capron.

He peered out into the darkness. From the ground, it definitely didn't look like Long Island. It shared no resemblance to the place where José had spent his summers, going to parks with his cousins with stolen bottles of vodka. José pulled out his phone. The battery hovered at 5%. He unlocked it and opened his photos, scrolling to a photo of Sarah and him. They looked so happy. *Why did she have to have been so goddamn cruel?* The more he thought about it, the more José blamed Sarah for this situation. If she hadn't cheated on him with Kyle Peterson, then he wouldn't have blacked out and fell asleep on the plane.

José stepped down from the plane. Beyond the dirt path, there were no signs of civilization.

In the distance, a light bobbed. José squinted, trying to make out what he thought was a torch. One torch became three, and in a few minutes, José could see three white men, dressed in frilly clothing, galloping towards him on horseback, brandishing rifles and lanterns. José tucked his pistol into his waistband and raised his hands.

The men slowed to stop around twenty feet away, aiming their rifles at José. A large, bearded man with a crooked nose spurred his horse forward and held out his lantern to illuminate José and the plane.

"From where do you hail?" asked the man in the thickest British accent José had ever heard. José took a step forward, "Capron."

"Capron?" the man eyed José warily, then the giant metal machine, "and this?"

José glanced back, "This is my plane."

"Plane?

"Like a car with wings."

"Car?"

José winced. *Another troop of maniacs.*

"A plane is a machine which can fly in the air. It accelerates super quickly and uses wings to lift off the ground." José watched their confounded faces. The man circled to inspect the other of the plane. "Does it flap like a bird?"

"Flap? No, no, it doesn't flap. The air pushes it up."

The man stepped down off his horse, nodding at his fellow soldiers. He walked cautiously towards José. "Show us."

José shook his head, "I can't. It's powered by gasoline and there's no more left."

"Gasoline?"

José sighed. This was already getting old. "Fuel. Like if that lantern runs out..." *Holy shit. Holy shit!* He smiled at the man, and said, "I can show you. I just need lamp oil."

The bearded man trotted along on his horse, José jogging besides, glancing back at his plane. The two other soldiers, left behind to guard the metal beast, had tied their horses to the wings and opened the door to explore the inside. José had argued for at least an hour to be allowed to stay while they fetched him the fuel, however there were three of them and only one of him. He was somewhat sure that all three had spotted the pistol sticking out of his waistband but must have not recognized it as a weapon. All he needed to do was get some kerosene from these lunatics, then he could continue his search for sane people.

José and the man passed through what must have been the most primitive village José had ever seen. Black and white men, women, and children, dressed in rags and caked in dirt gathered. A black woman, shackled to her stool, paused her dish washing momentarily to study the newcomer. Several hundred feet away from their path rose a fifteen-foot-tall stone wall along which torches hung at every twenty-foot interval. José wondered out loud, "What is this place?"

The bearded man grinned and exclaimed, "New York!"

June, 1681

Diane awoke with a start. She found herself inside what she guessed was a teepee. Strange, unidentifiable objects lined the canvas wall. On the other side, an unmoving figure lay on a small cot. Diane moved her head back and forth, feeling a cot underneath her body. She hoped the other figure was Chaska. Suddenly the entryway flap was lifted from the outside, light spilling in and blinding Diane. Her eyes adjusted to a kindly, puckered Native American woman holding a bowl of steaming liquid. The woman stared back, then said something in a language Diane didn't understand.

The woman closed the flap and approached Diane, who could do nothing but raise her head as her body still ached from the cougar attack. The woman carefully began dipping a cloth into the bowl of liquid and dabbing Diane's wounds. She was surprised at the soothing, tingly sensation that came from the substance.

After the woman left, the other figure murmured in Sauk, "Diane, are you okay?"

"I'll survive. You?"

Chaska grimaced, "I don't know."

"You don't know if you're okay?"

Chaska shook his head, "I don't know if you'll survive. We are hostages of the Shawnee tribe. They will kill us both."

Diane spluttered, "But that woman was helping us?"

"I have played unconscious for now. Sooner or later, they will discover that I am Sauk. Once they do, they will kill me and then you. Our tribes are sworn enemies."

Panicking, Diane retorted, "Well, then we escape!"

"How?"

Shit, he's right. Our injuries. I can't move. and neither can he...

'New York' was unfathomably disgusting. From a distance, it looked like a poverty-stricken hamlet with a poorly constructed stone wall that could tip over from a strong gust. As the bearded man, who had introduced himself as Thomas, and José neared the edge of the town, José could see that it was indeed a ghetto with decomposing battlements.

Men and women trundled miserably along, carrying bags of produce and rotting livestock. Many of the black people and some whites were chained up and scarred. José blanched at the sight of a prepubescent, emaciated, black kid with only one arm carrying a chicken cage across the street. The boy looked on the brink of death, yet the scraggly white woman who followed him prodded him harshly forward with the butt of a stick. Thomas leaned over to José and said, "How does Capron compare to the glory of New York?"

José said nothing as he his head began to throb with the realization that maybe Diane had actually transported him back to a bygone age.

Thomas and José entered a large two-story fortress in the city center, the only building in the entire city with more than one floor. Thomas pulled José towards a set of large open wooden doors through which Redcoats spilled in and out. "Step lively. The Colonel awaits you." A pungent odor accosted José's nose, a cross between sweat, shit, and blood.

"My god," gasped José.

Thomas nodded and smiled, "He awaits you, as well."

They climbed up a steep flight of stairs, sparsely decorated with swords, guns, and deer heads, leading directly into a large room that constituted the entire second floor. Compared to the rest of the city, this room was clean and manicured, yet still had an odor that made José want to retch. Colonel Richard Nicolls stood by the window, looking out over his city. He was short and muscular, mid-forties. The Colonel bounced with the grace of a gazelle to his desk at the sight of his arriving guests.

"Lieutenant!" he exclaimed, "what has ye brought me?"

Thomas took a step forward and saluted, "The culprit behind the great noise. This man claims to have been riding a machine called a 'planed'."

"Plane," corrected José.

"Ye mean to tell me this savage is responsible?"

"I'm not a savage!" exclaimed José. Thomas struck José across the face. José, stunned, clutched his burning cheek. The cold metallic feeling of his pistol in his waistband comforted him only a little. Thomas began explaining how he came upon the stranger and his magical flying device, concluding with the fact that José had asked for fuel. Upon hearing the final request, Nicolls leapt to his feet and proclaimed, "Preposterous! A crook, a spy! Be you Dutch? Spanish? A Catholic, I wager! They have been after our fuel supply for months. End him!"

Thomas moved toward José, drawing a blade from his belt. José whipped out his pistol and pointed it at the approaching man. Thomas, who didn't realize that pistols could be made completely out of metal, kept advancing.

"Get back!" screamed José, fearing that he would have to repeat this vicious act of self-defense. Thomas grinned, raising his knife to strike. José fired into Thomas's face, shooting a spray of brain, skull, and blood against the wall. His corpse thudded against the ground.

Nicolls reached for his desk, where he had a derringer hidden. José swung his pistol at Nicolls who was accustomed to sidearms taking at least a minute to reload. José fired a warning shot that whizzed by Nicolls' head. The Colonel hit the ground.

José made sure he had one more in the chamber before requesting, "Hands!"

Nicolls raised his hands quickly. "Stand up," José continued, "fuck with me and you'll be on the floor too!" Nicolls rose to his feet. José steadied his aim on Nicolls but glanced at Thomas' destroyed face and vomited. After enough had exited to calm José's nerves, he demanded, "I need as much lantern oil as you can give me."

"I...I can give you as much as you want. Yet, I require a token in return."

"What?"

"I'd like that firearm of yours."

"No chance."

Nicolls shook his head, "There've been two shots in the highest office of New York. My men are making their way here. You relinquish your firearm to me and I shall uphold your safety."

José didn't move.

June, 1681

Diane laid in the teepee, drifting in and out of delirium. From the last time the old Shawnee woman had tended to them, she could tell it was night. She was pretty sure that she had brought a watch, a cheap digital one, but it either fell off during her tussle with the mountain lion or maybe the old woman had taken it. The time travel device was thankfully still in her pocket.

"Chaska?"

"What?"

"Can you speak their language?"

Chaska sighed deeply, "Some words are similar. It won't be of any use. A Shawnee will kill a Sauk on site. And so would a Sauk to a Shawnee."

"We need to try."

The entry flap burst open and in rushed Chief Panii. The tribe's silver-haired, paunchy leader shouted an incomprehensible tirade and held out Diane's digital watch. In his other hand, he held a sharpened spear.

Chaska scrambled to say something to the Chief who paused. Panii asked what sounded like a question and Chaska nodded. The Chief lowered but did not drop his spear, circling Diane. He then said in Sauk, "I made a promise to my people that I would never allow a witch to walk our lands. I swore I would kill them. I swore that I would kill any Sauk that encroached on my home. But a witch is worse. A Sauk witch...your guts should be on the floor already."

"I'm not a witch."

Panii raised the watch and retorted angrily, "This is witchcraft."

"That is a...*watch*," Diane said 'watch' in English, "It tells the time."

"A pointless trick, you can tell the time by looking at the sun."

"This device allows you to tell the time to a very precise measurement."

Panii ran his fingers over the glow, "How does it work?"

"It goes from zero to twelve twice. Or to twenty-four once. Each number-"

Panii rattled his spear at Diane, the blade missing her skin by inches, "No, you miscreant! Where does the light come from?"

"The light comes from a battery." Diane knew what was coming next. She spent the next two hours explaining and re-explaining the concept of electricity, batteries, conductivity, and an entire list of related terms that could fill an introductory college class on electricity. She spent the next hour and half going over seconds, minutes, hours, days, weeks, months, years, and decades. Panii had gotten a horse leg to gnaw on during the second half, even sitting down on the ground at one point. Chaska asked a few questions as well. She realized how much she hated being a professor and how much education would be needed in the next few years for her plan to work. Finally, Panii was satisfied. "You're able to measure the time of a beating heart?" clarified Panii. Diane nodded.

"She has many other things. Things that make that watch look like an arrowhead," admitted Chaska.

Panii's gripped his spear, taking a menacing step towards Diane. She wasn't sure if he meant to kiss her or stab her.

José didn't lower his pistol. He kept it raised, albeit shaking, even when two soldiers entered the room. Upon seeing Thomas' body and Nicolls with his hands up, they leapt at José, but stopped short after Nicolls barked at them.

"Speak your piece," demanded Nicolls, who could see José's hand quivering.

"I already told you why I'm here. I need lantern oil, as much as you can give me."

"For what purpose? Does your sovereignty lack light?"

"I can use kerosene to fuel my plane's engine. If you give me a few barrels, I can show you how it works. The plane, err, the flying machine."

The Colonel yipped at the men behind José, "Smith, Benson. Fetch three barrels of whale oil and load them up on a carriage." Then, he turned to José, "I know not what kerosene is, we illuminate our colonies with oil from baleens. Would this work?"

José hadn't the faintest clue what the effect whale oil would have on the plane's engine, but he'd take what he could get. He nodded.

Nicolls continued, "Then you have my protection. Lower your firearm and let us go with haste to your device." José lowered his gun slowly but kept it visible.

José and Nicolls sat on a rickety supply carriage next to three large wooden barrels, each caked in oil stains and rust. Smith and Benson, walked briskly next to the carriage, shooting José dirty looks.

The two soldiers that Thomas had left, Blish and Doyle, were sitting next to the plane throwing stones at the hull, trying to outdo each other at making the biggest dent. Doyle kept claiming victory, so Blish threw his next projectile at Doyle. Right before a scuffle ensued, the two scruffy privates heard the wheels of the carriage, dropped the scrum, and stood at attention.

As they drew closer, Nicolls grew so entranced with the sight of the plane that a bit of slobber dripped out his open mouth onto the floor of the carriage. The carriage came to a stop a few yards away from the end of one of the wings. Nicolls, Smith, and Benson stared in silence at the plane. Blish and Doyle saluted Nicolls. Blish stepping forward, "Commander. We are hitherto unable to identify a thing inside-" Nicolls silenced Blish with a wave of his hand, then commanded all four soldiers to help unload the barrels.

"Where is the fuel required? And how soon shall it be ready to operate?"

José hopped down and gave a presentation on where and how to fill up the tank. Nicolls watched closely, still perched on the carriage. As the men moved towards the carriage to unload the barrels, Nicolls stopped them and then faced José with a devious smile, "These are three large barrels, costing the realm 5 sterlings per piece. We use them to light our colony, thus I would feel at ease with a form of collateral. Maybe, since foes we are no longer, your shiny sidearm?" José thought for a second and then handed over his pistol. He had used up all the ammo and was sure nobody here knew how to make proper modern bullets. Nicolls grinned as he ran his hands over the smooth metal surface of the pistol. The men toiled for the next half hour, clumsily centering the fat barrel spigots into the tank. Eventually, they used all three barrels. Checking the fuel gauge, José saw that the tank was half full.

The teenager stepped out of the plane and lied, "I can only take one other person." Nicolls jumped down from the carriage and presumptuously strode forward. Inside the plane, the Colonel watched carefully as José pressed switches and spun knobs.

"Ready?" asked José. Nicolls nodded, gripping his seat. As the motor turned over, any trace of precaution in the Colonel evaporated. José did not like the way the motor sounded, evidently the whale oil wasn't compatible. Nonetheless, the plane crept forward down the dirt path, slowly gaining speed. "I thought this was supposed to fly?!" shouted Nicolls.

As he pushed the throttle forward, José shouted back, "We need some speed first!" Nicolls' eyes grew wider as the plane traveled faster. They hurtled toward a line of large pine trees.

"Look ahead! Prithee, beware!"

José laughed and gunned the plane upwards. They soared above the treetops and into the bright sunny sky. José glanced over at the Colonel, who stared out at the landscape in dumbstruck awe, trousers wet.

"Are you peeing yourself?" José asked, disgusted. The Colonel pointed at New York, which now looked to José like a shantytown, "Fly over the city!"

José took the Colonel on a joyride up and down the coast. They would dive down on the Colonel's instruction to "inspect this" or "survey that." After an hour or two, José told Nicolls that it was time to return, as the fuel was running low, much less time than half a tank of gasoline would provide. The Colonel cheerfully patted José on the back. "You and I, old boy, shall ride upon the tails of angels."

⊕

Many hundreds of feet below, a gaunt, blonde, Dutch maid named Lotte stopped on the way back from washing her family's clothes in a river to stare at the giant roaring beast, cutting through the sky. Her soaking clothes hit the muddy ground as she sprinted away towards Fort Orange, the last remnants of Dutch colonizers in the Americas.

-

June, 1681

Chief Panii leered at Diane for a tense minute before growling, "What kind of things?" Diane swallowed, "Some are weapons. Some are tools. All will help your people not only survive, but poop."

Chaska cleared his throat, "Thrive."

"I thought my Sauk was bad," Panii paced back and forth, "The Shawnee are the greatest tribe this land has ever seen. Why would we need your help?"

Diane couldn't help notice the similarity between his rebuke and Chaska's, so she glanced over to her Sauk companion, who rolled his eyes. "When I say people, I mean the Shawnee, the Sauk, the Sauk, Chickasaw, Creek, Arapaho, Comanche, all of them. The whites have arrived, and before the age of your children, you will see destruction and death by their hands."

"You know this how?" growled Panii.

"Experience."

"The whites did this to your people?"

"Yes, Europeans did enslave my ancestors."

Panii raised his spear and laid the head on Diane's breast. She shivered at its coldness. Chaska grunted, tried unsuccessfully to stand, and fell on the ground. The chief chuckled and moved to the other side of Diane, keeping his blade pointed at her heart. "Why us?"

"Because your land greatly affects mine. Without the wellbeing of your land, justice will never be found in mine. I mean to unite the great tribes of the plains and those beyond in order to fight off the Europeans. Once you've accomplished this, they will respect you as equals and many, many lives will be saved."

"Why should I believe you?"

Diane met his gaze, "Nurse us back to health, then return with us to the Sauk Tribe."

Panii stared at her, his hand holding the spear, quivering. Diane closed her eyes, preparing herself for his decision. "If you do not believe me, ask him." The chief's hand stopped trembling and he removed the spear from Diane's breast. He crossed over to the middle of the teepee and knelt next to Chaska. "Speak, Sauk scum!"

It didn't take long for the chief to be intrigued. He instructed the medicine woman to heal them fully. After holding a tribal conference, his people were at first enraged that he was going to let a Sauk warrior and a witch live. They became even angrier when they discovered his plan to march to their enemies' camp. Panii related Diane's claims. After much back and forth, the Shawnee tribe coalesced, since despite their disapproval, Panii was still their ordained chief.

In the teepee, the medicine woman was just finishing up feeding Chaska and Diane. She departed, leaving the duo to themselves. "Diane, you had no right to invite the Shawnee to our camp."

"It's the only way."

Chaska sighed, "People say things are the only way when they don't want you to think about other options. You have yet to learn how we think and act. You will put my tribe in great danger."

"If this is not done, both tribes, all tribes, will perish."

"Are you from the future?"

Before she could answer, the medicine woman entered. Chaska shouted, "Get out!" and the woman dropped her supplies onto the floor and scurried away. Diane's cheeks burned. She knew answering truthfully could be disastrous. The more people who knew that she had time traveled, the harder she would have to work to keep history in check.

José's plane skidded to a stop on the dirt road. Hundreds of people, soldiers, men, women, and children, white and black, dressed in rags and frilly garments, had gathered on either side of the makeshift runway. *Word travels sur-*

prisingly fast here for somewhere with no SnapChat thought José, as he turned the engine off. Nicolls stripped off his urine-soaked trousers, grinning at José. "Well done! Fetch me some new trousers!"

Disgusted by the sight of Nicolls' disease infested crotch, José plugged his nose and handed the Colonel a pair of old jeans that happened to be in the back. Nicolls ran his fingers down the blue denim in wonder. "What is this material?!"

José shrugged, checking the plane's fuel gauge. They had burnt through several large barrels of whale oil in a worryingly short amount of time. While whale oil served as a temporary fuel, the engine wasn't designed for it and it showed. The sounds of the engine cooling down were worryingly rambunctious.

Outside a group of jumpy Redcoats cautiously approached the plane as if its nose could lash out and bite them. "Colonel? Are ye alive?"

The Colonel theatrically flung open the door, arms spread side to side. He paraded himself down the ladder, showing them and all the other New Englanders his new pants. "Never have I been more alive! I have seen the Earth from the heavens! Higher than the tallest peak. Faster than the quickest ship. With this, England shall be the crown jewel of the New and Old!" pontificated Nicolls, strutting for all to see, "the Dutch and the House of Habsburg shall crumble. Long live England and Charles the Second!"

At the mention of their king, the crowd cheered. José stepped down from the plane, and the people fell silent.

Nicolls turned to José. The Colonel clasped his hands on the teenager's shoulders, "They call this gentleman, José. Fret not, he is not of Spanish blood. He invented this device and he's the only one who knows how to fly it. He speaks our language well and will be considered by all a guest of royal decree!"

The Colonel's amiability astounded José, but he quickly realized that he was just a means to an end, the ticket to air travel.

"Give 'em a wave," Nicolls nudged José, who gave the crowd a peace sign. The people gasped and murmured.

"Are you quite mad?" demanded Nicolls, then explained that holding up two fingers was considered rude. José shrugged and the Colonel laughed, "No worries, my boy. We have much to teach one another. Now tell me, what other newfangled devices do ye have?"

Several leagues northeast, Lotte, the Dutch maid, rushed into a large cabin, followed by several surly Dutch soldiers. Anthony Colve, a stoic naval captain looked up from the multitude of maps detailing the New World laid out across his desk. His long curly hair bounced up and down as he rose to meet his visitors. In a thick Amsterdammer tongue, he reprimanded, "Military personnel only!"

The soldiers accompanying Lotte pushed her forward, and she stuttered out, "General Colve. My deepest apologies for the interruption. On the West Bank was I, when I heard a noise from above. I looked up and witnessed a giant flying object. It was making a sound unlike anything I've ever heard."

Colve took a step towards the girl, "Where was it headed?"

"To the outskirts of New York, I swear."

Colve raised his hand to his mouth, then ordered everybody but Lotte out of the cabin. He sat the maid on the other side of his desk and pulled out a large sheet of paper and a quill. "Tell me exactly what you saw," he instructed Lotte, who proceeded with a detailed explanation. Colve wrote down everything, his feathered quill whipping to and fro. After she was finished, Colve thanked and dismissed her. He then called Arend, one of his most trusted men, a tall, pale, pockmarked man in his late thirties, into the cabin. "Take this letter to Amsterdam on the next convoy and deliver it to the Stadtholder himself, no one else. Protect it with your life."

-

July, 1681

A month had passed before Diane could walk on her own. Chaska had been on his feet for a couple weeks, but was nowhere near his former fighting self. After hobbling around the healing tent for half an hour unsupported, Diane instructed Chaska and Panii that it was time to head to the Sauk camp.

Clouds filled the sky and light rain pattered down as Diane, Chaska, Panii, and half of the Shawnee tribe headed northeast. The company stretched far back, over the crest of a hill. Moccasins on the wet ground and jangle of bows and quivers made Diane's heart race with anticipation.

Diane kicked herself for all the things that had gone wrong. She was constantly sick with worry about her equipment stranded at the Sauk camp. God willing the tribe had been practicing her written language, but without her instruction they would have most likely bungled it. She would have to start from scratch. On top of all this, her only means of efficient travel, the airplane, was in the hands of a hormonal teenager. Diane had never felt so hopeless in her life. She caught Chaska looking at her. The wounded warrior quickly averted his eyes.

That evening, the brigade stopped to rest. They were halfway, according to Chaska's calculations. They would reach the Sauk camp the next evening. The Shawnee busied themselves with setting up camp. Many soldiers sat on the perimeter, monitoring the rapidly darkening plains like hawks. Diane, Panii, and Chaska huddled around a fire.

"Tomorrow, we will advance with both of you in front and make sure that you're very visible. I will not risk a surprise attack," Panii ordered, picking at his teeth. Chaska nodded, "Once we enter my lands I will make sure to announce our peaceful presence with a call."

Panii stood, grunted a goodnight, and departed to his tent, leaving Diane and Chaska to a suffocating silence. Hastily, Chaska stood and said, "We should both rest."

"In my time, I was a *physicist*," admitted Diane, throwing caution to the wind. She used the English word for physicist.

"What's that?"

"Somebody who studies matter and how it interacts with itself. I hated it."

Chaska sat slowly. Diane went on, "In my time, there's this thing called money, which controls everything. Hell, it controls everything in the east right now, but you'll learn that soon enough."

The warrior dearly wanted to ask what 'money' was, but kept his mouth shut.

"In order to make my venture possible, I needed people to help me pay for it. Those people gave me money thinking that I would help them accomplish their goals, but I decided that I couldn't bring myself to do that. They found out and came after me," Diane looked up at Chaska, "I don't think they'll stop until they find me."

Chaska rose, made his way over to Diane, and sat next to her.

"José?" he asked. Diane snorted, "No, not him. I didn't mean to bring him back. That's why he ran off. He hates me." Chaska comforted her with an arm around the shoulder and soon they were kissing.

The next morning, Chaska led the group the rest of the way, hollering a Sauk cry the entire way. By mid-afternoon, one of Chaska's tribesmen made himself visible a few hundred feet in front of them. He stood there, studying the brigade, unmoving.

"What's he doing?" Diane asked Chaska, who raised his hands high in the air. Chaska murmured to Panii, "Tell your people to do the same."

After the entire group's hands were raised, Chaska shouted, "Shappa! It's me, Chaska! We come in peace!" Shappa melted into the brush without saying a word. "What now?" Diane asked, unnerved.

Chaska shrugged and frowned, "No one from my tribe has ever done this before."

In New York, José had spent the last month taking Nicolls on joy rides around the eastern seaboard. The colonel demanded that José teach him how to fly, but each time Nicolls took the yoke José immediately had to take it back within seconds, as they would start losing altitude too quickly or Nicolls would lower the landing gear mid-flight. He had never met anybody as inept at piloting.

In a matter of days, every single person knew who José was. When he walked down the streets, most stared and whispered to each other. Several people, mostly the men, would approach him with an attempt at conversing, and then guffaw at his ridiculous accent.

The women looked at him with great curiosity. They were used to the gruff, unkempt men of the 1600s, so this handsome boyish celebrity, who was relatively clean as a whistle, would garner a flock of swooning female admirers anytime he walked through the streets. Being a teenage boy, José didn't fail to notice this, however he had seen enough of Nicolls' STD riddled crotch to steer clear of the opposite sex.

One particularly sunny day, José and Nicolls were flying over what would eventually be called Baltimore. They were returning from Jamestown, the British colonial capital of the New World, where they had given a demonstration of the plane to the major plantation owners and local government officials. They had also purchased several barrels of whale oil, which were to be delivered to New York on horseback. "I understand not, old boy, why you insist on transporting the whale oil by horseback. Let us carry the load on the flyer instead and be done with it!"

José rolled his eyes, "I'm getting tired of explaining this to you, the more weight we have on the plane, the more fuel we have to use."

"But the extra weight would be more fuel!"

"It wouldn't be in the tank. The oil we just purchased will get to New York in the same condition just as we flew it, and now we're not wasting it in our tank," snapped José.

Nicolls shrugged, not listening closely enough to understand. He peered out the window, "Would ye protest the release of objects from the plane in flight?"

José groaned. He had known this question would come up eventually.

The plane landed on the dirt road which had now been widened and smoothed out by José's instruction, making it the first official runway in the world. Lanterns had been posted along the ends and sides of the road in order to make night flights possible. A small hut off to the side had been erected in order to store extra fuel and the Colonel's ever-growing inventory of ostentatious flying attire.

José hopped out of the plane and stormed towards a carriage that had been waiting for their return. Nicolls followed, asking José if it was possible to drop cannon balls off the plane.

"José, my son, you forget yourself," said Nicolls as he followed José across the field towards an awaiting carriage, "I desire only to know if it's possible."

José snorted as he jumped into the carriage. Nicolls told the carriage driver to wait and leaned in close to José, "I may not be able to fly the plane, but I still control the fuel. Mistake me not."

⊕

Across the Atlantic, the Duyfken, one of the fastest Dutch ships and therefore one of the world's fastest ships, pulled into Amsterdam. Captain Colve's liaison, Arend, clutched the note detailing the flying machine. It had been a rough five weeks, filled with storms lasting days and a nasty bout of scurvy. Arend was glad to be back in Amsterdam, the jewel of the Dutch empire and his hometown.

After the boat docked Arend covered himself in a cloak and slipped onto the bustling ports, pushing his way through merchants and vagabonds from every nation imaginable. His childhood years as a dockhand flooded back, working an honest job during the day and committing petty crime at night. Even though Captain Colve had recruited him more than two decades ago, Arend still felt the most at home in these hectic canals. He scurried off the docks and bought a quick meal in a Frisian bakery, scarfing it down on his way to the Royal Palace, which loomed several miles in the distance. Amsterdam seemed dirtier and darker than he remembered.

He walked briskly along a canal, smiling provocatively at a pair of redhead debutantes in a riverboat. "Arend?" a voice behind him called. Arend swung around to see Dewitt, a tall balding man with eagle eyes and thick scar running from his left ear lobe to the corner of his mouth. Arend instantly recognized Dewitt, the infamous grandson of Johan van Oldenbarnevelt, founder of the Dutch East India Company or VOC for short (Vereenigde Oost Indische Compagnie). Dewitt had garnered a reputation of having the uncanny ability to be in multiple places at once and always three steps ahead.

"Mister Oldenbarnevelt. It's a pleasure to see you," Arend choked.

"Pleasure to see you as well, Arend. What do you have there?" Dewitt nodded hungrily at Colve's letter. Arend took a step back, preparing to run. He had promised to deliver the letter directly to the Stadtholder. Dewitt grinned, "You did not think that I wouldn't have eyes all over the ports that would tell me immediately that Colve's number one errand lacky traveled all this way to deliver news personally? Let me see what is so dire."

Two burly men appeared behind Arend and grabbed both of his arms. "Please, I must deliver this to the Stadholder first!" cried Arend, a huge mistake. Dewitt nodded to one of the men, who yanked Arend's arm forcefully at an unnatural angle, snapping it. Arend sank to the ground, whimpering. The two redheads who had been watching quickly took to their paddles and disappeared down an intersecting canal. Dewitt snatched the letter out of Arend's unbroken hand and unfolded it impatiently. Before he finished reading, Dewitt was already calculating how long it would take to prepare three of the VOC's largest ships to travel to the New World.

-

CHAPTER

10

July, 1681

Diane, Chaska, Panii, and the rest of the Shawnees stood in silence, hands raised. It had been five minutes since Shappa had disappeared into the brush, so Chaska decided to yell once more, "It is I, Chaska, son of Tacoda! Diane, the flyer, is here with us! The Shawnee with me are here on a peaceful pilgrimage!" Chaska knew that Sauk soldiers were listening from the bushes. Diane joined in, "The Shawnee are here to ally with you!"

They waited some more, before, one by one, a hundred Sauk soldiers materialized from the surrounding foliage, each carrying a knife or a taut bow. Mahka stepped forward, eyes blazing furiously, "We had assumed you had passed on to the next world. Here you are with an army of foes."

Seemingly unperturbed, Chaska nodded and proceeded to explain the events of the last month. Diane jumped in, urging the inter-tribal cooperation. The Sauk warriors lowered their weapons. Chaska shook his head. He opened his arms to Mahka who stalked off. Onawa appeared from behind a tree, beaming at Diane.

Panii and the Shawnee were still on guard, but more content that the Sauk weapons had been lowered. The chief took a step towards Onawa ceremonially and proclaimed in Sauk, "For as long as I can remember our tribes have been at war. It will require a great deal for me to be convinced that our peoples can put that history aside."

Onawa closed the space in between her and Panii, "You have seen the things that Diane brings?"

"Just one."

The elder woman grinned and replied in fluent Shawnee, "Follow me and I shall show you the tools of our salvation."

A thick fog rolled in. The Shawnee quickly began setting up camp around the southern border of the camp, where the gruesome Lacrosse game had taken place. The Sauk tribespeople sat in small circles, drawing on the dirt. Diane neared a group, looking down at what they drew in the dirt: her written language! All this time had not been for nothing. Diane fell to the ground in blissful tears, causing those around to check on her in concern. "No, no, you've been practicing!" she cried. Onawa pulled Diane up, "Of course, you told us our livelihood was at stake."

Onawa gave Diane a tour of the freshly educated Sauk town. Teepees had been set up as classrooms. The script had caught on like wildfire. Almost half of the adults and most of the children were now fluent. Storytellers recorded their stories on pieces of bark with little knives. Young ones transcribed their elders' stories with paint on rocks. They had even created a large message board in the center of the town by stretching several large buffalo hides tightly between two large totem poles. Diane watched, enraptured, as a group of tribespeople used sticks dipped in paint to scrawl their thoughts across the hide.

That night, around the flickering fire, Diane witnessed a young girl, Eyota, scribble "I love Boki" in the dirt. "Boki" was the little girl's brownish mutt that followed her around for scraps. Diane ran to open one of the metal boxes, snatched a writing pad and paper, and gifted it to Eyota, who immediately thought Diane was giving her extra kindling and she tossed the gift into the fire.

A commotion near the open metal box drew the attention of Diane, who sprinted back over. A young boy had grabbed a large industrial shake flashlight and inadvertently switched it on, frightening himself half to death, and dropped it back into the metal box. Diane lifted it out, making sure to close and seal the box afterwards. She would have to be more careful - one technological leap at a time.

As she swung the flashlight around, men, women, and children furiously dodged the beam. They were accustomed to artificial light being scalding. Soon the adults figured out that it wasn't harmful and laughed uproariously at the children who continued to flee the light that Diane whipped around. Even some of the Shawnee entered the camp to witness the gleeful commotion.

A cool breeze wafted the smell of feces and tobacco into José's small wooden cabin, which he had finagled after much debate with Nicolls. He had spent a few weeks inside the city walls, but the stench and attention drove him mad. A troop of guards had been stationed outside of José's cabin, with claims that it was for José's safety, however their blatant drunken aggressiveness made their real purpose clear. José was not a free man.

The interior of the cabin was simple. Several hemp carpets semi-covered a dirt floor. A small cot made of hay stood in the corner, with some of the scratchiest, rattiest blankets José had ever felt. He often found earwigs and moths crawling around the dense fabric. In the other corner, a wobbly desk sat next to a water bucket. José was never explicitly instructed on what exactly was the water bucket's purpose, but he used it to bathe himself, handing it to one of the annoyed guards when it was empty. On the desk, a large lantern balanced precariously, threatening to tip over at a moment's notice and douse José's abode into flames.

As an unwaveringly noisy chicken clucked outside his window, José distracted himself by tossing a polished wooden ball into the air and catching it. This mindless activity would have normally been excruciatingly tedious in any other time in José's life, but the simple action now soothed him. He still wasn't convinced that he was in the year 1681. He didn't trust Diane, Nicolls, anybody. They were all a bunch of lunatics upholding some elaborate ruse. But for what purpose?

A knock at the door pushed José to his feet. He slid the ball under his mattress. Nicolls entered without waiting for an answer, "Lad, to the flyer. We're off to test the drop."

The plane circled high above the dotted greenery. Nicolls pointed to a field a few thousand feet in front of them. "Keep her true. I shall open the hatch." Nicolls made his way to the back of the plane where a pile of different sized cannon balls sat in a wooden box.

José yelled, "Make sure you drop it well before where you want it to hit! We'll be giving it a lot of horizontal acceleration!"

Nicolls cupped his ear and shouted back, "What?"

José repeated himself, but Nicolls had just opened the door, drowning out any chance of conversation. They were a few seconds away from the field, so José violently waved his finger at Nicolls, who jovially hurled the cannon ball out the window. It hurtled down and slammed diagonally into the ground with an unsatisfying plop, sending several feet of loose earth in either direction.

Nicolls slammed the hatch close angrily, "What in the devil was that? Where was the explosion?"

On the next run, Nicolls dropped an even bigger cannon ball, and the same result occurred just with a louder plop and slightly more upturned dirt. On the proceeding run, frustrated as ever, Nicolls decided to chuck out a bottle of whale oil off the plane, despite much protest from José, who at that point, decided to land the plane back at the home landing strip. Nicolls was irate, "I understand not! Why doesn't it rain down hellfire? I only wish my foes to see that Armageddon hath come!"

José scribbled a list down on a scroll and shoved it at an approaching soldier, "Chill out."

Nicolls slapped the side of the plane and retorted, "Heat, you imbecile! Heat is the key! Not chill!"

The next day, José presented several bread-loaf-sized metallic cubes to Nicolls, who shook his head in disgust, chattering that the box didn't look like a cannonball, or any respectable projectile he'd ever seen.

On their first run of the day, Nicolls launched the cube out the window with reticence. The Colonel watched and José listened intently. After a few seconds, a small explosion flung dirt and rocks. Nicolls threw the hatch closed and started singing a sea-shanty.

That evening José showed Nicolls and some of his trusted men how to create a shell, fill it with explosive powder, and install a primitive contact fuse. The shell needed to be brittle enough to explode properly when landing on the ground but also not break while in the air. Gunpowder was not a novel invention for the British, but aerial bombing was quite revolutionary. The British, like all other naval European powers, used gunpowder in their cannons, but to put gunpowder *inside* the cannon ball had never occurred to anybody. José drew out a blueprint for Nicolls who raced off into town to start production. The Colonel had been spending so much time with José that several colonial lawyers had filed complaints with the civil office for a lack of oversight and gross negligence. The Colonel didn't care, publicly proclaiming that his time spent with José was sanctioned by the Crown. When the lawyers demanded proof, Nicolls offered them free trips on the plane. José felt like a ferry captain, entertaining an odd assortment of guffawing dandies.

When José wasn't occupied with these ridiculous tours, Nicolls dragged him on more and more runs, each time testing different sizes of projectiles. The explosions were getting bigger and so were the crowds of spectators.

José decided that he must find a way to leave this place, or at least Nicolls. He needed to continue his search for sane, civilized people. He needed to get somewhere that had cellphone reception.

Fifty miles north of Boston, three large Dutch ships set down anchor directly offshore. The crews from each ship piled into dinghies. Dewitt stood at the bow of the first dingy to arrive on the shore, leaping the distance before it touched land. With the shivering Atlantic and rising sun at his back, Dewitt grinned, eager to set out. Hundreds of Dutch, German, Polish, Turkish, Angolan, and Senegalese men, all employees and slaves of the VOC, worked tirelessly to shuttle weapons and supplies from the three ships to the shore. Dewitt swung his head southeast, almost expecting the flying machine to land directly at his feet like a loyal carrier pigeon.

-

November, 1681

From the roof of her freshly constructed cabin, Diane stirred a cup of steaming juniper tea with a small wooden carved spoon, while looking out over the noisy, burgeoning town of Cahokia. It wasn't really fair to call it "town" anymore, as a "city" would be more appropriate. Diane's cabin stood in the center, right next to the capital fort where Onawa and the Council of Elders met. The Council was the leadership system that evolved from the amalgamation of the Sauk, the Shawnee, the Iowa, and the Potawatomi, all of which had joined the coalition by moving their tribespeople into Cahokia, whose population was cusping on 5,000 people.

On the other side of Diane's cabin, connected by a small tunnel, stood a large shed, protected with metal grating. Inside were two direct metal laser sintering 3d printers and a connecting laptop terminal that Diane had brought along in the plane. All three devices were plugged into a power cord that ran up to Diane's cabin's roof, where a large array of solar panels soaked up enough energy to keep the printers and laptop going twenty-four hours a day. A padlock and two armed guards secured the entry to the shed, only allowing Diane to enter. She received shipments of ground up bronze, copper, iron, silicon, and gold ore that she used in the 3d printers to produce intricate mechanisms. This meant that the mining operation had to be scaled up, but with a large influx of able bodies moving into Cahokia each day, she had more than enough raw material. A large factory had been constructed in the city center, employing hundreds. For the first few weeks after it opened, it produced nothing but mining and harvesting equipment in order to jumpstart the acquisition of even more ore and raw materials. The next few weeks, books and other educational materials had flown out of the factory and been distributed among the flourishing three schools that had been established for all ages in different parts of the city. Now, the factory was producing record numbers of timepieces, mostly analog as Cahokia's power grid was still in its infancy.

Diane and the Council met every day around 2 pm to discuss plans for expansion, rollouts, production, and a myriad of other topics. In their initial meetings, they debated for hours whether to establish Cahokia as nomadic or solely agricultural. Many elders on the Council had failed to see a problem with the traditional system where tribes would utilize their current environment's resources to their heart's content and then migrate at the first sign of greener pastures, but Diane had hurriedly countered that an agrarian society would be able to better foster trades-men and specialized industries. These meetings had given Diane plenty of practice to clearly explain concepts. A for-eigner from an unknown land, a woman, with horrible Sauk, telling them what to do was preposterous, and her ideas made sense, which made it even worse. Diane was well aware of the Elders' feelings towards her. It was the same dynamic in academia where stuffy old professors hated to be corrected by a young brown woman.

She finished drinking her juniper tea and made her way down off the roof, telling herself to take it easy this meet-ing. She needed to give the Elders' a win or they would stop listening.

Diane walked towards the capital fort, a towering three-story building with traditional tribal pictures painted on every metal and wooden slab that made up the exterior. A massive 15-foot-wide chimney shot out from the center of the fort, surrounded by a large circular observational deck from which every corner of Cahokia could be seen. Diane shuffled through papers full of the day's itinerary as she walked towards the two large ornate doors, covered in in-tricate carvings meant to ward off evil spirits. Some of the pages had English written down on them so Diane could maintain an ounce of discretion during the meeting, and the rest of the text was written in Sauk, which had become the lingua franca of Cahokia.

"Diane?" prodded a familiar voice. Diane looked up to see Chaska standing at the entryway. They had only been able to see each other a couple times over the past few months. Diane had busied herself with creating an entire civil infrastructure and Chaska had been occupied with integrating himself into said infrastructure. Flustered, Diane let one paper slip out from the stack. Chaska, nimble as a fox, caught it before it hit the ground. He handed her back the paper and mumbled, "Onawa requested my presence."

Diane smiled weakly back at him. She already knew why Onawa had called him here, because Chaska was going to fulfill one of her items on the day's itinerary. The Sauk warrior followed the physicist into the fort.

Once inside, Diane greeted the Elders, nodded politely to Onawa and Panii, and took her seat in the chair circle that surrounded a large unlit fire pit. Chaska stood behind Onawa, placing a grateful hand on her shoulder. The walls were simple and the floor was dirt, no drawings and no frills. Wabaunsee, the shrewd Potawatomi warrior-chief, stood, stepped towards the fire, and raised a flint and steel. He began to sway and chant while he struck the steel over and over again. Diane caught him peeking at her peripherally to check if she was growing impatient, a mistake she had made in the earlier meetings. Diane tried to look as patient as possible, while counting the wasted seconds in her head. Finally, the fire was lit and the meeting commenced.

Diane stood and distributed hand-written copies of the itinerary to each Council member. Onawa read it carefully. Panii glanced at it tentatively and then started to fold the corners. Wabaunsee placed the paper on the floor without looking at it. Chaiton, the youngest of the Council, wispy hair on top of a waspy face, chewed tobacco as he pretended to read. These four, Onawa of the Sauk, Panii of the Shawnee, Wabaunsee of the Potawatomi, and Chaiton of the Iowa made up the Council of Elders.

Diane started to say, "First order of business-" but was interrupted by Chaiton. "Why is there a Sauk warrior here? Is this place not reserved for only those on the Council?" Chaska shifted on his feet, eyes cast downward. Before Diane could reply, Onawa cut in, "He is here on my behalf."

"Then I would like to bring some of my wives and their sisters," snapped Chaiton.

Onawa calmly replied, "I think we'd need a bigger building."

Panii and Wabaunsee chuckled while Diane hid her face behind her hand. Chaiton dismissed Onawa with a lazy yawn. Diane spoke up, "I believe the Sauk warrior is here because of number four on the itinerary." Chaiton quickly snatched up the sheet and actually read it, "Madness!"

Diane raised her hands in a diplomatic manner, "It's the fourth item on the list, which means that the three initial ones are more pressing. Number one, I think we should begin construction on an additional factory which solely focuses on the production of currency. We have to be careful about counter-"

Chaiton sprung up to his feet, "The Iowa took a great risk coming here to join this nonsense because we heard of the great advancements which would bring peace among all the tribes, but a unified military is just another means to oppress our people. Already, we speak Sauk! We live on their lands! I've lived long enough to know that corruption of power is inevitable. Have you learned nothing from the Cahokia of old?!"

Diane nodded calmly. "Fine, if you want to leave, leave. I understand if you do not feel comfortable with the changes I have brought upon you. Good luck convincing your people to devolve back to their old ways once they get a taste of the future."

She leaned forward, her eyes growing narrow, "The Iowa are but a drop in the ocean. Thousands of other tribes will join us. The changing of the tide is inevitable and so is this. So, go, depart from Cahokia. When you come crawling back, begging for protection against the Europeans, we will welcome you with open arms."

The other Council members and Chaska watched him until, with a deep sigh, Chaiton fell back into his seat. Diane softened, conceding, "I realize this must all be difficult. A foreigner comes in and tells you how to change your entire culture. I am and will try my very best to preserve your traditions and beliefs, but time is of the bladder."

Chaiton brightened and erupted with laughter. Onawa rubbed her forehead, while Chaska hid his face. Then, the mighty Iowa chief filled the fort with great breathy whoops, falling from his chair. Panii and Wabaunsee started to dance gleefully. Diane's cheeks grew red and she wondered what word she had accidentally said instead of 'essence.'

Her blunder relieved most of the tension allowing the rest of the meeting to go quite smoothly. Diane was able to get permission for a new currency mint, reserve several acres of land in the surrounding area for livestock and grains, increase silicon mining, establish the need for a unified military, and submit a proposal for a Cahokian constitution. The Council members accepted the first three items with ease. When Diane revealed that she wished to nominate Chaska as their military general, Chaiton exploded once more. He made many counter-proposals, most of them ridiculously unproductive and laughable, but finally they were able to come to an agreement that the Iowa tribe would make up a special-ops force that would be led directly by Chaiton. The final item, the proposal for a Cahokian constitution, was nearly fifty pages long, so Diane passed out copies and told everybody to carefully revise it. She would take their notes after a week's time.

After the closing ceremonies, Diane rushed out of the fort, a thousand and one things on her mind. She barely heard Chaska catch up to her and say, "I can't thank you enough."

Diane kept walking, "Don't thank me, it was Onawa's idea."

"Well, I still appreciate it. I won't let you down," Chaska replied, desperately. Diane wanted nothing more than to drop everything and drag him into her cabin, but she knew that it would just complicate things. She slowed only slightly, "I would hope not. Cahokia's fate hinges on you doing your job."

Diane scurried away towards the southwest of Cahokia where she was scheduled to meet with representatives of the Lakota tribe and then, directly after, survey a possible site for a printing press. Chaska watched glumly as she blended into the mid-afternoon traffic of downtown Cahokia.

-

May, 1682

A gigantic, content heifer munched calmly on the patchy grass in the middle of the target field, surrounded by massive divots from previous bombing runs. A leather rope secured to a pole kept the cow in place. José and Nicolls stood off to one side. "What think ye?" asked Nicolls. José shrugged, a little disturbed that Nicolls had woken him up at the break of dawn and dragged him out to face the living creature that they were about to annihilate, "Yeah, it's a cow..."

"The grandest bovine in the Western Hemisphere! Twice the size of any in New York, I bartered her from some Quebecois toads. Magnificent, eh? If this proceeds as planned, the crown shall have no other option than to send support," babbled Nicolls. José blurted, "The Crown?"

"I wished to parley with you on this subject. If Virginia's interest is piqued, then news and discussion of the flying machine has been bouncing around London for weeks. When we relocate to Jamestown, there shall be royal representatives present. These are men of stature and not to be trifled with. They expect a full demonstration and inspection."

José took a sharp breath in, "Fine. Why a cow? I mean, if we're able to blow up a small house, I'm sure our bombs are effective against people."

The Colonel ignored José's plea for bovine clemency, "Ye must give me an ear. I have revealed that the word of the flying machine is known in Britain, thus it is known in other places, most assuredly in our adversarial sovereignties. Ye must know that England is beholden to ye, just as ye are to it. Do not forget this."

José scratched his head and looked once more at the cow who looked up at him with seemingly mutual concern. Nicolls' baroque English confused José, especially when the Colonel talked about some other group of lunatics. No matter, José wouldn't be subjected to Nicolls and his inane plots for much longer. He had just thought up a plan, and the cow was a vital part.

It took a carriage thirty minutes to travel from the target practice field to the runway outside of New York. The carriage, which was horse drawn of course, went at a casual pace, so José estimated it would take a cavalry fifteen minutes at most. As Nicolls' men loaded up the last of the bombs, José sat behind the wheel and closed his eyes.

Nicolls skipped into the cockpit, wearing the jeans that José had given him with a white frilly blouse.

As the plane leveled off, José noticed a crowd of Redcoats scattered around the edges of the target field. By the door, Nicolls jumped up and down like a sugar-high kid at a waterpark. José brought the plane down a few feet and made the three-fingered gesture to Nicolls to open the door and ready the bomb, which the Colonel did. Wind whipped into the cabin, flapping Nicolls' frilly blouse. José checked his seat belt and gripped the wheel. After weeks of practice, Nicolls had perfected the timing and knew exactly when to drop the bomb in order to hit a specific spot. He screamed at José, "Leftwards!" José nodded and adjusted his line.

On the ground, the spectating soldiers pointed and cheered as the prop plane zoomed towards them. The cow looked up uninterested and went back to munching on some delicious dandelions.

Just a few more seconds.

As Nicolls hefted the bomb out of the door, José twisted the body of the plane right, but kept his line straight, so that the open doorway was now an open floor beneath the Colonel. Nicolls didn't grasp what had occurred until he was half way down, the ground rushing up towards him. It wasn't the ground that killed him, it was the cow. The bomb, which Nicolls had dropped seconds before he was thrown out of the plane, had detonated directly next to the bovine, killing it and propelling its bones and guts into the air at a fatal speed. The Colonel's falling body met with the upward meaty projectiles, which would have made for quite the spectacle if anybody could have seen it, but a cloud of dirt disguised the event from all. The Redcoats had seen somebody's body flailing from the plane, but there was little evidence of who it was. Several minutes after the explosion, while the soldiers were milling about, investigating the scene, one private found a patch of lacy muddy cloth stuck inside a cow heart ventricle.

After a few minutes of heated debate, the Redcoats came to the consensus that it could be Nicolls' white frilly blouse, stained by the detonation. A moment of pensive silence filled the air. José's plane was nowhere to be seen. They raced to their horse and galloped back towards New York.

José had just landed his plane on the runway, but left the engine running. Blish and Doyle, now permanently assigned to the runway, scrambled over to the plane door, ready to attend to their fearless leader. José opened the doors, red and sweaty.

"Where's the Colonel?" asked Blish. Nicolls had instructed them to never let José fly the plane alone. The teenager stepped down, rubbing the back of his neck, trying his best to hide his trembling hands, "He wants me to do another run. Unfortunately, I'm out of gas, and he wanted to stay at the range to see the damage of the last run closer up."

"Did it work?"

"Yeah, like a dream. Cow's a whole bunch of pieces."

Doyle and Blish nodded to each other, hurrying towards the supply cabin. José waited until they had their backs to him before anxiously surveying the surrounding land-scape for signs of pursuit. He shouted after Doyle and Blish, "The Colonel wants to do the run several more times, he requested that we have enough fuel, cause he doesn't want to waste any more time. Bring some extra barrels?"

Doyle and Blish stopped abruptly. They had never taken orders directly from José, who was gulping a lot and stealing glances into the forest. "I don't want to piss him off, do you?"

The two dolts conversed quietly, pointing to José and then to each other. Finally, Doyle asked, "How many do you need?"

"Seven."

José ran up and helped them load the seven barrels onto the cart. Doyle and Blish began to argue about which one of them should ride the draft horse, so José hopped on himself and spurred the massive, huffing beast forwards. They reached the plane, José hopped off and flung himself upon the fuel nozzle. After the second barrel was emptied into the tank, José threw down the funnel and opened the door to the plane, "That's enough for now, let's put the rest inside."

Doyle and Blish were confused. "Shouldn't we put in three?" inquired Doyle. José shook his head furiously, now sure that he could hear the sounds of the cavalry, "No, no, no! Two's fine, let's go!"

"You hear that?" Blish asked Doyle. Doyle nodded, stepping around the plane to get a better look, "A goddamn stampede!"

"Please! Focus!" pleaded José, who tried to lift one of the barrels himself. Doyle and Blish had lost all interest in helping José and moved to the other side of the plane to watch the incoming parade of Redcoats. José threw himself once more upon the fuel nozzle, this time closing it shut. He leaped into the plane, locked the door, and plopping into the pilot seat. The fuel gauge was disappointingly low, José wouldn't even be able to make it to Pennsylvania. He needed those extra barrels. The Redcoats were shouting indistinctly at Doyle and Blish who looked up at José through the windshield in astonishment. As the Redcoats surrounded the plane, Doyle and Blish started picking up rocks and chucking them against the windshield. The plane's door began to rattle, and José scrambled back to check that it was secure. He paced back into the cockpit. His fingers hovered over the ignition key as he contemplated just mowing down the Redcoats and their horses before serious damage was done to the plane.

A bullet ripped through the door and embedded itself in the far side wall. This was all that José needed to turn the ignition key. The engine sputtered, trying to turn over. José ducked down as more musket fire echoed outside. Strangely enough, no new holes appeared on the plane's hull. José crouched underneath the seat, hyperventilating. He listened intently to shouts of "Ambush!" and "Formation! About face!". Battle cries from the Redcoats sang out, however, in minutes an eerie silence fell.

José gathered his wits and raised himself up to peek out the window. Dead British soldiers and horses scattered the runway and the adjacent fields. José couldn't make out a single living being. He tried to look quickly in the side view mirrors, but both had been shattered in the onslaught. The sole church in New York rang its bells furiously, sounding the alarm. José heard footsteps approaching the side door. They seemed cocksure, patient. A leisurely knock on the plane door made José flinch and knock the seat, sending the pilot's headsets flying.

"Now there, I just saved your life. At the least, you owe me the pleasure of thanking me to my face?" said a deep male voice in English with a Germanic accent. José thought for a second, assessing his options. He could turn off the plane and surrender or he could gun forward and try to make it far enough to escape. Still, the remaining barrels of whale oil were outside. He turned off the engine and crawled towards the door. He put his trembling hand on the lock, but did not unlatch it. "You're not going to kill me?"

"Once again, I just saved your life. I lost two men in the process. Why would I kill you? Diminishing returns. Please step out before more soldiers arrive, I'd hate to have to kill them all as well."

José's brain told him to keep the door locked, but something about the collectedness of the voice on the other side made José's hand throw the latch. The door swung open revealing Dewitt and around fifty men all shapes and sizes, armed to teeth. They had positioned themselves behind the plane, but faced New York, readying themselves for reinforcements. José squinted at Dewitt, "Who are you?"

Dewitt smiled and extended a bejeweled hand, "Your biggest aficionado."

-

CHAPTER

13

May, 1682

Diane had around forty things she needed to take care of before lunch. Blissful ignorance was a distant, fantastical dream. Diane had become addicted to work. Even in her down time, which was a few dismal hours at night, she found herself toying on the computer in the 3d printer shed, trying to perfect the next advancement.

In much less time than predicted, Cahokia had become a fully functioning democratic oligarchy. The population had grown to a permanent population of 8,000, with an additional 3,000 to 4,000 visitors at any given time. Word of this technological oasis had spread faster than many actual wildfires throughout the American Midwest and the Great Plains. Tribal visitors would trek far distances to Cahokia and leave with clocks, tools, watering systems, solar powered lights, bicycles, hundreds of types of medicines, the Sauk written language, and many more wonderful *inventions*. A new currency, which Diane had named 'Fuzi', was being printed in enormous amounts and distributed at a furious pace. There had been a lot of resistance and misunderstandings with the Fuzi, since all tribes were used to bartering, so a currency was an often-frustrating concept. Many didn't see the point and refused to acknowledge its value. Diane implemented a law that all businesses must only accept Fuzi as payment. She knew that it was impossible to enforce this, but once Fuzi caught on just a little, Diane was sure it would take off.

There had been several aggressive tribes, like the Apache and Ute, that had attempted to raid Cahokia, but were quickly driven off by Chaska's military force, like a bunny trying to attack a bear. Outfitted with quick-load guns, binoculars, armored clothing, and progressive tactics, there wasn't a tribe in the northern continent that could scratch Cahokia.

The new Cahokian constitution was only a few weeks old. It was, in practice, just an outline to be filled in. The only laws that had been agreed upon in the initial ratification were how other laws would be created. There were no longer just the original four tribes, the Sauk, Shawnee, Iowa, and Potawatomi. Eight more tribes had joined, the Cree, Cherokee, Dakota, Arapaho, Kiowa, Chickasaw, Comanche, and Pawnee. There were members from other tribes that lived in and visited the city, but per the constitution, a tribe could only be represented in the Council of Elders if they had at least five hundred permanent residents in Cahokia. This was kept track of by a hardworking, detail-oriented census bureau whose employees Diane had trained personally. Obviously, the acceptance threshold to allow a tribe into the Council of Elders would eventually have to increase for a growing population, but Diane had provided the department a formula.

The twelve elders would meet every day at 2pm, another written law. If one wasn't able to be present, they must send a representative. Once a session began, the Council could propose laws and amendments which could only be passed after a full write up of the proposed change was approved by each member of the Council. It wasn't a perfect or particularly speedy system, but it was fair, or at least gave the appearance of being so.

After the system was established, the Council and its constituency brought on an onslaught of proposals, some of which made Diane's hair stand on end. Integrating spiritual rituals, deemed essential by and to the Natives, into a system of laws seemed somewhat irrational to Diane. All drugs were legal. Diane supported this, however Diane did not support their law which required the Council to take certain drugs at least once a month. She had never taken any psychedelics in her life and was particularly sick of the Council's practice of taking Peyote during the full moon. Diane would melt into herself, not knowing where or who she was. Polygamy and polyandry were legalized. Diane suggested better rights for women, but the almost completely male Council had vetoed her. Even Onawa, the sole female Council elder, had been reluctant to pass these. In their revisions, the elders had stripped women of the ability to work in certain industries. Diane had protested fiercely but to no avail.

Taxes, or tributes as they were called among the tribes, were one of the first contentious issues. Panii, Chaiton, and Houso, the Arapaho chief were enraged that other Council members could have the chance to receive their other tribes' money, however Onawa soothed them with the fact that they would be getting at least twelve times the amount of tributes respectively.

With increased silicon mining, Diane was able to produce thousands of new solar panels, with which, after receiving the Council's permission, she began to construct a power grid and street lamps along all major roadways in Cahokia. This was the first widespread instance of electricity in Cahokia (and the entire world). Cahokians and their visitors were awestruck. For the first several weeks of lights' installation, gobs of people could be found crowding around the base of each street lamp, staring deep into the glow like it was a portal into another dimension. Some believed that it was a doorway into the realm of the Great Spirit so they began camping out directly underneath these street lamps, causing massive traffic jams. After a little educational campaign, Cahokians lost interest, but visitors still were entranced by them, so Diane and the Council created a department whose sole purpose was to make sure people weren't loitering underneath these marvels.

After marking the new day on her calendar, Diane hustled out of her cabin and down towards the central square where a large dirt space was surrounded by two-story wooden cabins and open teepees. A gathering of hundreds filled the square, beating drums and dancing in ceremonial garb. Fifty or so men and women were tied up to posts, some moaning in pain from cramps, some twitching from dehydration, and a few screaming for help. An crowd of Cahokians watched from the perimeter as Shamans, with black-paint covered faces and pierced lips, wandered the human forest, every once and while poking a prisoner with their staff. The Council of Elders had passed a law that Shamans could act with spiritual license among the general population, giving birth to an emerging caste system. Murder was technically legal if proved to be for the greater good of Cahokia.

Feeling like small minnows in a suddenly big pond, the Shamans had banded together to create a religious organization. Diane wanted to call it a church, but no actual building had been built or mentioned. The Council has just passed another law that the Shamans must send one representative to their 2 pm meetings, so the position of Head Shaman was created. The Shamans were in the process of choosing, and the Council expected a new member soon.

The event in the square was called *Ordeals*, a witch trial that had been brought to Cahokia by the Comanche and Kiowa. If a person was accused of being a witch, a Shaman could order the person to be tied up for eight to nine days straight. If the man or woman survived the trial, they would be set free with a clean rap sheet. The percentage of accused people who survived pleasantly surprised Diane, however she still questioned the trial's effectiveness.

She was heading towards a large plot of land on the outskirts of eastern Cahokia that would be perfect for a large-scale hospital. Diane had brought several petabytes of medical data on several drives, full of blueprints and instructions for equipment, basic medicines, and procedures, diagnostic and surgical.

Diane entered the Eastern district of Cahokia, the most densely residential neighborhood. Since most tribespeople were used to living with their extended family members, a hired crew of at least a thousand able bodied Cahokians constructed large cabins. These wooden buildings were two stories, a great novelty, and had a gated-off backyard area, in which families had fire-pits, animals, or teepees. Diane had designed the cabins, originally estimating that it could hold 20 people maximum, but her faithful census bureau had reported that there was an average of 30-40 people living in each one, with little complaint.

East Cahokia seemed alive with youthful vigor. Hordes of screaming kids barreled by Diane down the street. The sounds of their shouts blended into those of an even bigger gang of children on the next street. Diane grinned from ear to ear, pausing for a quick second to watch the crowd of kids toss a small giggling boy, no more than 5 years old, around in the air like he was a baseball. Women, babies, and elders watched from the surrounding cabin windows.

Diane heard cries and shouts in Sauk, Shawnee, Dakota, and some other tongues she couldn't identify.

"Mother, you're going to be late." Diane spun around to find Nikan, her assistant. Nikan was the most masculine woman Diane had ever met. Growing up as a Comanche warrior, she could break a man's neck with her bare hands, or at least claimed to be able to. Like most Great Plains veterans, Nikan had scars all over her body, the most gruesome of which ran from underneath her right breast all the way up to the base of her left earlobe. Her nose was crooked and her eyes small. Her mind was sharp, which was why Diane had handpicked Nikan from Chaska's army. Nikan spoke every language that could be found in Cahokia, even a few words in English, French, and Spanish. Diane never had to explain anything twice and Nikan loved the long hours. She was the perfect protege, with the one exception that she had an annoying habit of calling Diane *mother*.

"You brought all the binders?"

"Every single one, mother."

Diane pivoted on her heels and marched as fast as she could away, trying to catch Nikan off guard. As usual, Nikan was comfortably in stride with Diane. "Did you remember to follow up with the Shamans?"

"They're sending Gujek. He'll meet us there."

Diane nodded her head sarcastically, crudely imitating a Shaman, which sent Nikan into a giggle fit. Her laugh was the most feminine thing about her, and Diane couldn't help laughing herself at Nikan's breathy snorts. Another even larger kid parade blocked their path, so Diane and Nikan quickly rerouted down a path between two backyards. In the one to their right, a family squatted around a fire, eating large slabs of Bison meat with their hands. In the one on the left, an older woman rode a teenage boy who Diane assumed was autistic. The boy was squealing in delight while the woman worked furiously. The neighbors, who were in plain view of this disturbing display, were quite uninterested, unlike Diane who couldn't do anything but watch. The smell of the bison steaks wafted over, and she scribbled 'Save Bisons' on her notepad.

Diane and Nikan reached the empty plot on the border by the very last houses. A hundred feet past the empty plot was a patrol, all on horseback and dressed to the nines in combat gear. They saluted reverently to the two women as they passed.

A handsome man with a black-painted face and large talons piercing his lips, ears, and nose, approached lethargically. "Shaman Gujek!" Diane smiled and bowed. Gujek clasped Diane's hand in his, closed his eyes, and started muttering prayers.

For the last week and a half, Shaman Gujek had been the presumptive choice for the Shaman's representative for the new Council seat. Diane surmised this because the Shamans sent this blathering idiot to every meeting she had been to in the last week and half that required religious oversight.

"Thank you," Diane cut off Gujek who had just begun his second verse, "Let me tell you what we want to build here."

"A spiritual safe haven for those who have fallen out of The Great Spirit's grace?"

"It's a good guess, but it's actually a *hospital*," Diane said, "A giant medicine tent. To heal the sick and disabled."

"The way of the Great Spirit has served these great tribes for thousands of years, kept them safe and just. The Shamans will grant permission for this endeavor but only if our traditional methods are carried out within its confines."

Diane pretended to mull this over, "No. I respect your traditions but the methods that I can bring will be much more effective." Gujek pursed his lips and crossed his arms. Nikan stepped up, "She means no insult to the Great Spirit, she only wishes to use the tools that Wakan Tanka has granted her."

Gujek rubbed his right pointer and middle finger on his chin, nudging the long talon that dangled down to his chin, "What kind of procedures would be done here?"

Nikan listed on her fingers, "blood draws, vaccinations, spinal correction, casts for broken bone-"

"I can personally promise you that by next year, most newborn babies will survive. Nine out of ten," Diane cut in. Nikan and Gujek stared at her in amazement. Gujek stuttered, "Nine out of ten? Can you guarantee this?"

Diane nodded assuredly. Gujek recomposed himself, "The Shamans will not like to be usurped from their divine positions, especially when it comes to..." Gujek faded as a group of three warriors on horseback approached the trio from the perimeter. They didn't move to get down from their mounts. The center warrior, a lean, middle aged Sauk man announced hurriedly, "There's a commotion in the Southern markets. Chaska was called, but he requested your presence immediately."

Diane and Nikan climbed behind two of the warriors, clinging tightly. In a split second they were gone, replaced by a cloud of dust. Gujek coughed, swore violently, and trudged back into the city.

Galloping at full speed allowed the warriors to reach the southern markets in ten minutes. Just as the eastern sector of Cahokia was mostly residential, the southern sector was commercial. Bartering went down in a vast jungle of booths and tents that were so hemmed together that it appeared like one giant seething complex of canvas. A layer of smoke from fire pits and tobacco constantly rose off the roofs, obscuring the covert business deals and meetings from the outside world. Diane and Nikan slid off their rides onto the ground. The pudgy warrior pointed northeast and said, "You'll find Chaska around thirty booths in that direction."

Diane and Nikan sprinted through the bustling market, leaping over people, carts, large animals, buckets full of every type of spice available in North America, and rowdy gambling games. The dense air trapped underneath the canopy irritated Diane's throat as she panted heavily. The market was organized like a giant spider web. There was a large open space in the middle where a constant sea of traders yelled cheaper prices at each other. Hundreds of paths extended off from the center, twisting and intersecting, creating a maze so unbelievably hard to navigate that the Council had decided to employ a small army of guides to help lost shoppers. Many merchants lived full time in the market, which was technically illegal but barely enforced.

Angry shouts in Sauk, Pawnee, and a strangely familiar language drew Diane towards the emergency. It was on the other side of the line of booths, so Diane smiled at a cowering woman, non-verbally asking for permission for passage through her tent. The woman bowed her head so Diane and Nikan barreled through, bursting out into the adjacent pathway. Chaska and several of his soldiers surrounded three white men, dressed in dark traveling coats, muddy breeches, and unkept wigs. They're faces were poorly shaved. They had no exit, as Chaska's men blocked any means of egress. All three were talking in cascades of furious French. Diane took a deep breath and raised her hand to greet the nearest Frenchman, a gruff, pig-faced man. He muttered something to his two similarly bedraggled companions.

Diane had taken many years of French and had even lived in Montreal for a year, but after years of focusing on Sauk and never opening her Duolingo app, her French chops were rusty. She stumbled through an introduction, "Hello, my friends. Welcome to Cahokia. Please, my French is very bad. Speak slowly and clearly."

The men collectively sighed in relief, finally somebody who could speak their *langue native*. The gruff explorer adjusted his wig and replied slowly, "Thank the gods. We thought we were going to leave here in a box. It's heavenly to see a soul blessed by our tongue. What is this place?"

"You are in Cahokia, capital of the Cahokian Empire. My name is Diane. And yours?"

"Daxton Mathieu," Daxton nodded to the other two, "Jules and Marin. Are you a woman of Christ?"

Diane shook her head, eying the muskets attached to Daxton's belt. "Tell me how you arrived here." She maintained a cool, diplomatic tone.

"Fur is our trade. Some of our clients are groups of sav-Indians farther east. Quebec is strife with them, so beyond purely financial endeavors, a large part of our time is spent introducing them to the Good Word. You must allow me to regale you with the glory of Jesus."

Diane shook her head. Daxton gulped, "Well, your kind kept mentioning a great mythical mecca to the west with riches beyond our imagination. We had to come see for ourselves."

Diane gestured toward the market center, "Please, follow me."

A hushed silence followed them everywhere, followed by an explosive buzz of conversation after they passed. Children fled with terrified squeals. Diane cautiously led the three Frenchmen westwards out of the market. They entered one of the central roadways that acted as a spinal cord of Cahokia. A good fifty feet wide and straight as an arrow, the dirt highway extended all the way up to the northern tip of the city. The mob of people moving up and down in all different directions paused for a second to inspect the motley Europeans, who spotted a defective street lamp that decided to turn on during the day. They became moths, jogging over and staring directly into the bulb. Nikan intercepted a pair of anti-loiter enforcers who were headed straight for the trio of ignorant foreigners. Diane sidled up to Daxton, whose mouth was hanging so far down, she could have stuck her entire fist into it.

"It's called electricity and it's not magic, nor the work of God. It's science."

Jules, a greasy, unkempt frenchman continued to stare up as he replied, "Science is nothing but the study of God's miracles."

Diane deflated. There was no point in arguing about divinity, especially with Gallican Catholics. "Imagine the roads of Versailles paved with orbs of light? We'd be granted dukeships! Louis would kiss our feet!" cried Marin, youngest and least smelly of the three, to his salivating partners. Daxton ripped his eyes away from the light to Diane to plead desperately, "Where did you obtain this? We must know…"

"It originated here, in Cahokia," Diane glanced at her watch, "This is not what I wanted to show you. Come, please, quickly."

It took several more minutes of prodding to drag the white men away from the light, but finally, Diane and Nikan were able to transport their visitors to the western neighborhood of Cahokia, colloquially known as *The Asha*, short for *Aashaa Monetoo*, or the *Good Spirit*, in the Iroquois language. There weren't enough Iroquois tribespeople for them to have representation on the Council but they were well regarded by most as the best farmers in the land. Hundreds of Iroquois lived in the Asha and tended to the plantations. They had learned the new farming technology quickly, and, for this, had become a powerful minority.

Diane, Nikan, Daxton, Jules, and Marin stood on the precipice of a short drop into the dirt. In front of them lay the Asha in all its agricultural glory. Fields of tobacco, quinine, potato, peppers, tomato, corn, beans, squash, and pumpkins stretched out over the horizon. Each field had at least one large solar-powered tractor bumping along, either tilling, fertilizing, or harvesting. Even Diane felt her skin shiver and her chest tighten.

"Where are the draft-animals?" Daxton broke in.

"There aren't any. Cahokia harvests its crops with machinery powered by the rays of the sun."

The group was silent for several more minutes. She faced the Quebecoises and said kindly, "I know this may be a shock to you. Cahokia is not a city of savages. You are welcome here whenever you please." Diane switched to Sauk and asked Nikan quickly, "Go get the new rollouts. Three of them." Nikan disappeared like a specter. The three Frenchmen continued to stare out at the expanse.

Daxton choked on his next words, "This place...this city is a marvel. The world needs to, nay SHALL know about it.

If we were to return, would an exchange be possible? Would the sa-...Cahokians deal with outsiders?"

Diane scratched her chin faux-thoughtfully, pretending that she hadn't rehearsed this conversation a hundred times before, "In time, with the right relations established, yes."

"What other wonders do you have?"

"Here come some now."

Nikan appeared, rolling two objects, both covered by hemp blankets. Behind, a scrawny teenage girl rolled a third. The objects were propped up against a bush and the pubescent helper scampered off after giggling some obscenities about the men to Nikan in Lakota. Diane walked over to the closest object and whipped off the blanket. Daxton, Jules, and Marin inhaled sharply in unison. Two metal wheels in a line, one in front, one in back, were connected by a metal triangle. The hypotenuse was parallel with the ground. On the front end, a bar perched perpendicularly with the triangular frame and wheels. On the back end, a pear-shaped blob of rubber sat with its fat end pointed backwards. The shorter bar intersecting the two wheels had a round metal gear, on which hung a chain that was connected to the rear wheel. Two flat boards, no bigger than a child's hand, shot out at supplementary angles from the gear.

"What does it do?" asked Daxton. Diane grinned, swung her leg over the frame, and pedaled away. The three Frenchmen glanced at each other and then all sprinted over to the two remaining hemp-covered objects. After a scuffle, Marin and Daxton claimed their prizes, Jules pouted hysterically until Diane returned and handed hers over to him.

At first, the men, like toddlers, failed to realize that forward movement was essential to not falling down. Marin caught on first and began zipping up and down the flat border of the Asha. Daxton and Jules got it soon after, following each other in dangerously tight circles.

The area between the Asha and the rest of Cahokia was a sparsely populated industrial zone, with three manufacturing plants and two processing plants. The nearest processing plant, which focused mainly on root vegetables, had an outdoor patio where workers could take breaks. Concurrently, there was an increase of squash which had caused a small panic in the factory, and workers were forced to work overtime. With little regulation on work-life balance, many of the employees were exhausted, one being Kostini, a short-tempered, Chickasaw with a droopy face and a bum leg. Kostini had been a stellar hunter before getting his calf ripped apart by a mother bear. When his tribe had decided to relocate to Cahokia, he had fought to remain independent. He hated his new job. At this moment, Kostini had just snuck out from his shift and was discontentedly puffing on some tobacco.

Marin, who was still joyously riding his bicycle, veered off from the edge of the Asha and down into the industrial zone. The Frenchman lost his balance as his tires hit uneven ground. The front wheel slammed into a tiny gully formed by runoff water from the processing plant, flinging

Marin through the air directly towards Kostini. Marin slammed into Kostini's back, causing the lit tobacco to spray everywhere, burning both men. Marin screamed, and Kostini, who had just spent the last twenty-one hours mindlessly laboring, thought that the conquistadors finally had come to invade Cahokia. Without a second thought, Kostini drew his potato shearing knife and sliced Marin's throat.

CHAPTER

14

May, 1682

"Demount, young sir. I want to shake your hand," said Dewitt coolly, "I'm not a man who likes to waste time. The Britons have sent for the reinforcements. Hark, the bells tell us that. Follow my lead and you shall live to see another day."

Dewitt flicked his decorated index finger at New York, like a omniscient conductor. Sure enough, faint sounds of hoofbeats could be heard under ringing church bells. Dewitt twirled his finger again and his men began loading their guns. Scores of them hid behind trees, while the rest scuttled underneath dead Redcoats and pretended to play dead. Within twenty seconds, Dewitt, José, and many exhausted horses were the only visibly living things in sight.

Once again, Dewitt implored, "Step down, young sir, I promise I will not harm you."

José stepped down, unable to think of an alternative. Dewitt strolled over to a dead Redcoat and retrieved his pistol. José gulped and his heart skipped a beat, but Dewitt simply held the pistol out to José, handle first.

"Unload it, make sure there is nothing."

José checked the empty chamber. He nodded to Dewitt, who smiled back, snatched the gun out of José's hands, grabbed José, pulled him into a headlock, and aimed the gun at José's temple. This was done so quickly that José had trouble realizing what happened until Dewitt murmured under his breath, "Do forgive me, they won't shoot first with you at play."

The New Yorkers charged towards the pair, surrounding them and the plane. They leveled their guns at Dewitt from all sides, huffing angrily and spitting obscenities. These were reserve soldiers, continuously on call to help in cases of emergency, however, by virtue of being reserve soldiers, many were unseasoned and poorly trained. The utter defeat of their first team unsettled their commander Samuel, who would have retired long ago if he was from José's time, but his years of experience of lucking his way through wars against the Spanish, French, and Dutch gave him an edge and a particularly nasty prejudice against anybody who wasn't born under an Anglo-Saxon regime. The commander urged his horse forward a few steps and faced Dewitt with the most ominous glare he could muster.

"Release our flyer and ye shall have a choice of the tightness of your noose," scolded Sammie. Dewitt responded in a language which José thought might have been Russian but was actually Lithuanian. Sammie rubbed his brow, trying to remember if the few words he had learned during the Thirty Years war were Lithuanian or Polish. Dewitt seamlessly switched to Lower Prussian, which confused Sammie because it sounded like German with a potato in the mouth. One of Sammie's cadets, a waifish man named Gerald from Northern Wales, had spent some time in Bavaria, so he hailed Dewitt the best he could in German. Dewitt immediately switched to fluent Turkish. The men began to shout at him angrily, telling him in colorful ways to shut his dirty continental trap. Sammie shouted over the din, which only spurred the rest to raise their voices. They were all so busy trying to decide which hurtful names to call Dewitt that they failed to notice his men rising from the dead and slinking out from the surrounding trees. Dewitt pushed José to the ground just as Sammie's men noticed the ambush. José listened underneath Dewitt's knee to several poorly aimed shots from the New Yorkers and enough perfectly aimed shots from Dewitt's men.

"Again, my sincerest apologies. Let me to dust you off," Dewitt lifted José to his feet, cleaning off the latter's jacket.

The Dutchman's soldiers had Sammie and four remaining Britons pinned. Their hands were raised, and from the smell, it was apparent that at least one of them had shit themselves. Sammie's right arm was bleeding profusely. José tried to speak, but all that came out was a large glob of spit. Dewitt nodded sympathetically, patted José on the back, and moseyed over to the shivering captured New Englanders.

"In my many years of corporate servitude, I have learned one important thing. Wealth overpowers the nation, every time. My men work for a living, not because they feel obligated to. Those who I employ fight for me because they have found an outlet for their blood-thirst. You fight for the crown. Dying for Charles is pointless. Monarchs change castles faster than vagabonds change alleys. Already, the Merry Monarch had dissolved your piddling parliament for the fourth time. He's unfit. I smell a revolution and yet here you all are rotting away in a faraway land while your commonwealth falls apart."

Sammie chuckled, "I know a corporate whore when I see one. This is not Cambodia! You want political discourse? What do you think William shall think of this? Do you think his marriage with the Duchess of York, that bloody whore, is enough to salvage a war between our two countries? Money is all that matters to you, yet ye attack a British colony with no regard for what it will do for your stock?"

"Quite right," said Dewitt to Sammie, then spun on his heels and marched over to José, who was still standing in the same place where Dewitt had pretended to hold him hostage.

The Dutchman patted José on the shoulder, "What's your name?"

"José..."

"Are you Spanish?" Dewitt asked in fluent Castilian Spanish.

José shook his head.

"Well, you obviously understand Spanish. Where are you from?"

"...Capron."

"Where is that?"

"Um, to the west."

"Over land or sea? How far in your flying machine?"

"Land. Several hours."

Dewitt took out a long tobacco pipe and lit it snappily with a match, "Capron, eh? I've been told of large nations in the South and Central Americas, but never to the West."

He shot a large grey haze into the air, before extending a hand out to José, "I must impart my deepest apologies, my intent has not been to bamboozle you. Dewitt van Oldenbarnevelt, at your command. I come from the Low Countries." José found his hand in Dewitt's. The dutchman continued, "Help me with something. When we arrived, the Redcoats were firing upon you and your craft, but the fearless captain over here demanded that I step away from 'their flyer'. Were you under their protection?"

"I...I was...but I may have murdered their Colonel."

Dewitt suppressed his glee, "And, pray tell, why did you slay him?"

"I just want to go back home. I needed to come back here to get more fuel."

"José, I'd like to help you get back home. What might I do?"

"Help me refuel the plane?"

"Certainly! I only request that you take me with you. I would be forever in your debt, and trust me, of all the people in the world that you would like to be indebted to, I am the best choice."

José only thought for a second. He would prefer to not travel with more lunatics, but it was impossible to refuel without help. The barrels were simply too heavy. Dewitt squeezed José's shoulder once more like an old friend, and wagged his finger at a group of VOC men. "Refuel the flying machine. He'll show you how."

As José and the men funneled the remaining barrels into the plane, Dewitt marched back over to Sammie and leaned in close, "I can tell you have never spent any time with the Jews of Amsterdam. You were correct in the fact that VOC stock will plummet. When it does, I will use my liquidated savings and dividends to wax my shareholding. Hell, maybe I'll even give a hint to some of my associates. Then when I reveal that I have taken control of the flying device to my stockholders, we will mass produce it on a large scale. The VOC will not only rule the seas but also the skies. More importantly, our stock price will soar, and I will have made hundreds of percent on my initial purchase. Selling the short, but I can't expect lowly English swine would understand. So, I beg of you, tell Europe this was the VOC."

Dewitt gave a little condescending slap to a speechless Sammie. The VOC men holding the Redcoats at gunpoint moved quickly in and dragged their hostages back to the walls of New York.

"Are you prepared to fly?" Dewitt asked as he neared José, who nodded. The Dutchman added, "Wonderful, my second mate, Manuel will be joining us."

At his first glance of Manuel, José choked. Manuel wasn't striking in any particular way, with the sole expectation of looking scarily similar to José's father's favorite professional football player, Deion Sanders. José had never been a big football fan, but Angel's life-size poster framed in their kitchen was standing in front of José with a leather tunic and a large nest of dreads.

José wanted to lie again that he could only take one person, but Dewitt didn't seem as stupid as Nicolls. He wiped his chin, and tried to think his way out, "What about the rest of your men?"

"They have other responsibilities. There are other celestial devices in Capron?"

José shook his head. Nicolls and his colony of lunatics had been torture, but at least this lunatic would allow him to finally return to normal civilization. Perhaps, José told himself, he could get on a talk show with Dewitt and write a book about his experience with this isolated insane asylum. He'd fly west for a while and hopefully pick up a signal.

"Give me a brief moment, then we may depart," The click of Dewitt's boots brought Martijn, a salty Dutch mercenary with a missing hand, scampering up. Dewitt grabbed the back of Martijn's neck and ordered in their native language, "Visit General Colve. Deliver him the news post haste and then sit on him. Gather as much whale oil as you can. Go!"

Martijn was gone, along with the rest of the men, leaving nothing but a giant pile of dead British soldiers.

"After you," said Dewitt, motioned for José to board, which he did, then Manuel, then Dewitt.

José shut the cabin door. He brushed by Dewitt and Manuel, "Find a seat."

As the plane's engine sputtered to life, Manuel slid into the adjacent seat, then spoke in a deep, sub-Saharan accent, "Teach me."

It wasn't a question. José pressed the throttle and began rotating the plane. The plane's landing gear rolled over several dead Redcoats, jiggling the cabin up and down. "Buckle your seat belt."

"Seat belt?" Manuel looked at the roof and walls of the cockpit. José did his own so Manuel followed suit. Dewitt gripped a strap hanging from the ceiling of the cabin and peered out a porthole. The plane moved faster and faster, down the makeshift runway, then soared up. Dewitt felt his own net-worth soar along with it. He laughed, giddy and uncontrollable. Manuel joined in, smacking José's chest playfully before singing a string of piratical chants in Portuguese. Even José felt the corner of his lips rise.

-

CHAPTER

15

May, 1682

Marin held his hand up to his neck as blood flowed through his fingers. Kostini, satisfied with his work, stood with purpose and marched into the factory.

Inside the factory, a few hundred men and women prepared potatoes, carrots, and corn, tossing the finished crops respectively onto three long conveyor belts. A flutist and a drummer played in the corner, giving the workers a rhythm to match.

Kostini entered, proudly planted his feet, and yelled, "The whites have arrived! To arms!" There was a hurried scramble to the door, all followed Kostini outside. Marin's corpse was still oozing blood from the neck. The workers began arguing about where the next whites would come from, where to go, who to tell, betting on who could kill more, until Miwo, the factory manager quieted everybody down with his booming voice, which was the very reason he was given the job as factory manager, "Okay, okay! Well done, Kostini, however policy dictates that we inform the nearest military patrol. Jorbu, Halona, Aiyana, Wayra, and Citali, go in different directions to find the nearest soldiers. Everybody else, stay here and stand guard."

A few brave workers grunted that moving as a pack would be safer, but Miwo silenced them with a glare. He bent down to the dead European, Kostini joining him with a grin. "Pretty good cut, right? I learned how to do that from the Buffalo war."

"Shut your dirt-infested mouth," spit Miwo, who was Cree. Several decades previously, the Chickasaw and the Cree had gone to war over a particularly large herd of buffalo. The Cree had been losing badly until they decided to partner up with Choctaw and decimated half of the Chickasaw warriors in a nocturnal ambush. Then the remaining Chickasaw warriors raided the camp of Spanish explorer Hernando De Soto, killed him and his crew, and took their weapons and supplies. Using their new-found loot, the Chickasaw avenged their fallen brethren, dicing up the Cree and the Choctaw. Needless to say, tension between all three tribes was still running high.

"Yes, sir," responded Kostini, and poked both of his index fingers up by his head like horns, the hand signal for Buffalo. Miwo leapt on Kostini, pummeling him. Half of the workers cheered him on, while the other half let the fight go on for a minute or two longer before pulling the enraged, beet-faced manager off his beaten-to-a-pulp employee.

"Get back to work, all of you! Who is in command here?!" yelled Nikan at the top of lungs. She shoved her way through the riff raff, but stopped dead in her tracks, staring down in horror at blood-soaked Marin.

"Which one of you did this?" Nikan cried. The workers collectively turned to Kostini, who had just wheezed back into consciousness, his face almost as bloody as Marin's. At that moment, Daxton and Jules cycled towards the factory, finally getting the hang of their pedal-driven mounts. Diane skipped behind them. The two Frenchmen skidded to a halt a good twenty feet away from the crime scene. Daxton squeaked out, "Marin?"

The factory workers put two and two together. They fled back into the factory and down alleyways. Daxton screamed, pulled out his pistol, and fired at the retreating Cahokians. Jules reached for his holster but lost his balance and clumsily tumbled off his bike. Daxton scrambled over to Jules, yanking his fallen comrade's pistol out. Breathing heavily, he took aim at Diane. Jules cowered on the ground, nursing his bruised leg.

"All a ruse, eh? You bring us out here, give us gifts, then pick us off one by one?" spit Daxton, "Signed your death warrants, you have! The Sun King shall march upon this wretched Gomorrah and then you-"

The next syllables that exited Daxton's mouth were full of blood as Nikan jumped the distance between them and shoved a blade cleanly through Frenchman's throat, from one side to the other. Daxton gurgled incomprehensibly for a few seconds, tottered around, and then collapsed to the ground. Nikan turned to Jules, who had been watching this unfold with wide horrified eyes. Nikan took a step forward, extracting another blade from somewhere in her vest. Jules closed his eyes, quickly muttering a prayer to the Almighty.

"Nikan, enough," Diane commanded in Sauk, finally having shaken herself out of her state of shock. Nikan stopped advancing, but stared at Jules, daring him to attempt an escape.

"We have to kill him. He will tell others," stated Nikan.

"We've screwed up so much...oh, Nikan..."

Jules could tell that Diane and Nikan were discussing his fate, so he pleaded his case pitifully, "Please, please, please, spare me! I shall not bring anybody here, I swear! I shall implore my regent for a swift departure from these lands at once, never to return! Oh, please, my children, my wife, my beautiful wife! 'He shall wipe away every tear from their eyes, and death shall be no more, neither shall there be mourning, nor crying, nor pain anymore, for the former things have passed away!'"

Over the babblings of the terrified European, Nikan went on, "More will come. We hide the bodies and his friends think they died on the road, by wolves or another tribe. You don't want this traced back to Cahokia."

Diane shook her head, "They did nothing wrong! He did nothing wrong!"

Jules continued rocking back and forth, "The Lord is close to the brokenhearted and saves..."

"Who asked you to start all this?" Nikan questioned Diane with a deadly calm demeanor, "You bring us all this, then chastise us for protecting it? You claim the Whiteman is our enemy, then you protect them when they come here?"

"I'm sorry, Nikan, I'm not used to violence like this."

"You know, many wonder where you're from, why you're doing this. Where are you from, mother? Why are you here?"

"Nikan, enough!" She pulled out her pistol, pushed past Nikan, aimed at a screaming Jules, and fired. The back of Jules' head exploded, spraying red and white all over the dirt. "Clean up these bodies and meet me outside my cabin."

Diane trudged away from the scene, hiding the tears rolling down her face. Nikan gazed after her departing superior.

Hours later, Diane trudged into the Council meeting, avoiding eye contact with any of the twittering chiefs. Her mind was playing the gory spurt from the back of Jules' head over and over. She barely noticed Onawa coming over to talk to her.

"Great Spirit be with you. Have you made a decision?" Onawa asked tenderly. Diane looked up, doe-eyed, "Decision?"

"About the *sewage* system. Copper or plastic?"

Diane hadn't given it any thought, "Plastic."

The Chiefess could tell that something was amiss, Diane wasn't her sharp, wordy self. It would hopefully make things a lot easier. Onawa cocked her head at Panii who returned the gesture affirmatively. Panii whispered in the ear of Toyah, the formidable Comanche chief with a close cut mohawk. The rest of the Council members picked up on these signals and found their seats. Silence and tobacco smoke pervaded the room. Diane almost got up and began the day's itinerary but stopped herself when she remembered that the Council still needed to go through the pre-meeting ceremony. When nobody got up to chant, Diane grew nervous. Toyah and several others' glares bored into her. When Chaiton snapped something to Houso quickly in Arapaho, a language that they knew she didn't know, Diane was positive she was in trouble.

Diane rose from her chair, articulating her defense, "Where I come from, there is peace. It is so prevalent that violence, of any kind, is seen as an offense to the Great Spirit. When I came here, I was shocked at the violence, but don't take my words as a true evaluation of your societies. This morning, three Frenchmen arrived in Cahokia. These were the first of many to visit our city. I don't blame the factory worker. It may take me a while to acclimate to your cultures but I will never abandon or betray you."

Toyah waved his arm in the air, his giant bicep jiggling back and forth, "I, for one, am extremely pleased to hear all this, and we can all agree that your Sauk has gotten really good." All of the Council members burst out in guffaws and cackles. Cheeks burning, Diane crossed her arms, not liking that the chiefs laughing at her was almost becoming a tradition during these meetings. Onawa wiped tears from the corner of her eyes, "We're not going to let all this progress go to waste because you were reluctant to kill a white man." Onawa's face grew serious along with the rest of the council. Diane's grin vanished. Onawa took a looming step towards Diane, "But, if you ever talk badly about the Great Spirit again..."

The Council burst into laughter once again. A few elders were rolling in the dirt. Onawa rubbed her belly, deeply satisfied, "We're thankful for all that you've done. However, there is one problem."

Diane shut her eyes, waiting for the punchline. Onawa continued, "You've changed us from nomads to farmers, and we see the reason, but we also see the effects on the land. Our numbers reach the tens of thousands which we believe to be unsustainable. What would you think about starting a new city?"

"A new city?"

"Cahokia can expand, yes, but your goal is to unite as many tribes as possible, right? There are many more tribes out west, too far to travel here. If we established another city farther west, we could connect the two cities with smaller outposts along the way, promote trade, spread our technology faster, and recruit more."

Diane was thrilled, but worked hard not to show it. She had planned to unveil the very same idea of a second city in just over two years, after having enough time to convince the Council of its utility, but they had brought it up first. Now, Diane could temper her reaction and make demands.

"I'm not sure that's the best idea at this moment. Our technology will allow us to grow more sustainably and we don't want to spread ourselves too thin, too quickly. What exactly did you have in mind for the trading route?"

José turned the plane more northwest. Manuel watched him carefully, absorbing every movement of the wheel and every knob or button pressed. Dewitt riffled through the aft compartments, speed reading manuals full of complex jargon and bouncing repair parts in his hand. A gear wrench slipped from his hand and toppled to the floor, clanging loudly.

"We need everything in one piece!" José shouted back. Dewitt picked up an old wrinkled 1980 Sports Illustrated Swimsuit edition that José had stolen from his father. Dewitt smoothed out the cover, ogled Christie Brinkley, then dived into the contents of the booklet. The pages were full of hyper-realistic depictions of scantily-clad wenches. The drawings looked so real that he had to restrain himself from trying to grab a handful of flesh. Dewitt turned to ask José where one could find these shapely maidens when he noticed something even more shocking. In the top right corner of the cover page, underneath the large bold title, was a date: *February 4th, 1980.*

"We're about an hour out," announced José. Dewitt shoved the magazine into his tunic and approached the cockpit. The plane glided along the bottom of a large dark cloud which sprayed moisture onto the aircraft's windshield. Manuel murmured something to Dewitt who nodded and tapped José on the shoulder, "Let Manu have a go."

"A go? A go at what?" José adjusted the yoke down to avoid the sloping cloud cover.

"I want to steer," Manuel said offhandedly. José immediately shook his head. He still had nightmares about Nicolls trying to fly the plane. "No fucking way. It took me years to learn how to do this."

"I have a knack for captaining vehicles," returned Manuel, who eyed the yoke eagerly.

"I don't care. You could kill us."

"If it wasn't for us, you'd be dead, remember?" Manuel said with a slimy grin. José understood the message clearly and let Manuel take the yoke. He could always just grab it back if they went into a nosedive.

Manuel delicately took control. José glanced at Dewitt who winked back. José tensed, ready to spring into action, but Manuel was a natural. José couldn't believe his eyes. Only after a few hours of watching somebody else fly, Manuel had learned how to comfortably maintain altitude and coast on currents. José was pretty sure Manuel even checked the fuel gauge at one point.

"I met Manu when he outmaneuvered three of my fastest ships with nothing more than a fishing scow. He used a cannon to disable one of my galleon's rudders, how I still haven't the faintest," reminisced Dewitt. Manuel smirked, pulling the plane into a graceful banking turn, adding, "The gods were favorable upon me that day."

"The gods!" Dewitt jeered at Manuel, "I regret hiring a polytheist as my second mate, but he's decent enough to hide it when we're around pious investors."

José didn't really understand what any of that meant so he moved his head up and down and said, "Yeah." His confidence that he was still in the year 2019 shrank a little bit more.

Several hundred miles in the distance, Lake Michigan glimmered dully against the grey sky. José leaned forward and audible gasped. Slightly more west than where Chicago would be, lay a large city, with farmlands, factories, buildings, and rising smoke. José whisked the yoke back from Manuel who, along with Dewitt, gave no protest as they were too busy matching José's dumbfoundedness at the sight of the metropolis. Dewitt asked "That is Capron?"

José didn't really know how to answer.

Chaiton and Houso stood up nervously. Even though they had rehearsed their pitch on trading routes several times in the last weeks, Chaiton had always freestyled his speeches and Houso felt terrible from a long night of opioid abuse and too many squash breads.

"A road from Cahokia to-" said Chaiton and Houso at the exact same time. They paused and glared at each other, before doing it once more. Chaiton cussed out Houso who dejectedly took a step back. Chaiton puffed out his chest, "A road from Cahokia to an additional city would have endless possibilities. Transportation, let us dive-"

Chaska and four of his highest-ranking soldiers stampeded into the room, cutting off Chaiton. The warrior-general b-lined for Diane and whispered something in her ear. Diane tottered to her feet, mumbled an excuse, and bounded out of the room with Chaska and his men. The Council members gathered their belongings and pursued, wanting to see whatever had gotten their nervous wreck of an advisor more riled up than usual. Chaiton threw his hands up before running after the others.

Chaska led Diane towards the border of eastern Cahokia. His entourage, which had grown to a dozen soldiers, trailed behind a few paces, making sure no citizens were following. Diane couldn't see anything in the distance besides the familiar spots of piney forests and rolling emerald hills. "How far out?"

"About five or six borels east," replied Chaska. A 'borel' was the standard unit of measurement of distances that had evolved in Cahokia and was equivalent to a quarter of a mile. "We first spotted them through binoculars, and came immediately to you, but I kept soldiers out here to maintain their landing location."

"You haven't approached yet?"

Chaska shook his head. Diane waved over four of Chaska's soldiers and commanded, "Split up, circle round the machine on either side and secure it from the east. Do not kill the inhabitant, but he will most likely be armed. Stay there until further instruction. Go!"

The four warriors quickly returned each with an electric motorcycle especially designed for stealth patrolling. The four diverged into two pairs and hummed away eastwards. Diane motioned for the rest of Chaska's entourage to come close for a little powwow. Sufi, a lithe, sunken-eyed killer gave her binoculars to Diane.

She scanned the horizon, finally spotting three figures approaching the city on foot. From this distance, she couldn't make out their faces. The plane was nowhere in sight, most likely behind a slope.

"Everybody but Chaska, maintain a quarter of a borel behind us, but make sure that you're visible to our visitors. No sudden movements, do not hold your weapons out, but be ready to use them."

Diane then cornered Chaska, "We'll be speaking in a language you won't understand but I'll let you know any pertinent information."

José's face had turned a light shade of green, his forehead creased and sweaty. His lips moved urgently, silently mouthing to himself. Dewitt tried for a second to read his lips, a skill he had picked up attending Royal ceremonies and VOC shareholder meetings. Manuel trotted behind them, transfixed on the urban sprawl. He stopped, hearing something. Dewitt grabbed José, "I've learned to stop and wait to see what Manuel hears."

"What?" José had been lost in his own thoughts.

"There is...something, out there. I've never heard it before," Manuel whispered. Dewitt pointed towards the city earnestly, but Manuel shook his head and pointed to the left and right. "It's almost like a swarm of bees but much faster."

Dewitt stepped closer to José, "You've never been here before, have you? This isn't Capron?"

José took a deep trembling breath that failed to calm him, "It's not."

Dewitt exchanged several words with Manuel in an unknown language before saying in English, "Proceed." The trio resumed their walk to the city. They traversed a small glen, passing a group of tree stumps. Manuel ran his fingers over the smoothest tree stump he'd ever seen, then noticed the finest sawdust on his fingertips. As they exited the last bit of trees between them and the city edge, they saw around a dozen figures a good half mile away. After a moment's hesitation, on Dewitt's demand that they not appear fearful, the three recommenced their walk.

May, 1682

"José, where have you been?" asked Diane in English.

The pilot chuckled nervously, avoiding eye contact with Chaska, "Let's talk, just us two."

"Who are your friends?"

Dewitt proclaimed, curtsying with a flourish of his right hand, "Dewitt van Oldenbarnevelt, and the esteemed Manuel Da Silva." Manuel bobbed his head politely.

Diane furrowed her brow. The tall white man, most likely Dutch from his accent, spoke with great authority. The other man closely resembled a famous football player whose name escaped Diane. It was going to bother her. "Welcome to Cahokia. Where are you from?"

"South Holland, but I reside wherever the wind takes my company. Manuel is from the sandy shores of Angola."

Diane groaned internally, fearing José had brought a high statesman of European capitalism to Cahokia. "José, where's the plane?"

"It's close," offered José, while taking note of the line of warriors behind Diane and Chaska, "Can we?"

Diane walked with José away from the group. Chaska turned his glare onto Dewitt, who whispered to Manuel, "You wouldn't happen to be familiar with any savage tongue?" Though Manuel had been to many continents and countries, this was his first time in North America. He began a series of greetings in every language he knew, which only drew confused looks from Chaska. Manuel gave up after introducing himself in Basque-Icelandic.

Meanwhile, José and Diane's discussion soured. "I'm starting to think that you actually sent me back in time," hissed José. Diane pinched her nose, "Of course, I never said otherwise."

"You gotta get me back! I don't belong here!"

"You can make a great life here, José. Cahokia is a great city, full of modern technology. You can help me bring humanity through a glorious revolution long before-"

"You crazy bitch! You stole my life away from me!"

Diane took a step back, raising her hands in defense, "Calm down."

"You're from the future, you know how to get me back!" screeched José, grabbing at Diane. Chaska barreled into José at full sprint, knocking the scrawny nineteen-year-old to the ground. José cradled a bruised arm, whimpering.

Diane chastised Chaska with a disapproving glance. Diane knelt down, talking quietly to José so that neither Dewitt nor Manuel could hear, "The way I see it, you have two options. You could live in Cahokia, forget the future that will never come to pass, and help me grow the present. You'd be one of the most powerful people in the world, with anything that you want at your fingertips. Or, you could continue with this temper tantrum, leave Cahokia, and get lost in obscurity."

José wiped his nose with the back of his hand, collecting himself, "You're not going to help me get back?"

Chaska could see Diane's nostrils flaring and her face began to flush a deep red. José pushed himself defiantly onto his feet, meeting Diane's gaze with sudden steeled serenity, "If you won't help me get back, I'm going to destroy everything."

Diane's anger boiled over into clenched fists and spit, "You don't want to go to war with me, José."

"And if I tell my buddies over there what year I was born in?" Before the last word had left his mouth, Diane was clutching his collar, trying to cut off his airway. Manuel took a step toward the commotion, so several of the guards extracted their pistols. Manuel raised his hands and retreated.

José's face began to grow purple as Diane's grip squeezed tighter. He didn't struggle, his arms hung loosely at his side, almost as if he wanted her to go tighter and take his life. Diane released him, "Telling them, or anybody, would bring you nothing but pain."

"And your friend here doesn't already know?" José asked bluntly, rubbing his aching throat. Diane didn't deign answer.

José watched rays from the setting sun outline the Cahokia skyline, then turned and flicked his head at Dewitt and Manuel. The trio began the walk back to the plane. Diane got the attention of the soldiers and touched her ear. Sufi held up a small metal radioing box to her ear and relayed the command.

Dewitt and Manuel walked a few steps behind José, wordlessly arguing. Finally, Manuel spoke up, "We're not going into the city?"

"We have to leave," José replied after a tense beat, "We're not welcome here."

Dewitt halted, snagging José's shoulder indignantly, "I came all this way under the supposition that we were going to see the birthplace of your flying machine. I will not return empty handed!"

"That place is not the birthplace of my plane!"

"Then where is?"

"I'm not sure..."

"Are you a liar, a coward, or both?"

Manuel perked up, listening. Dewitt squeezed the pilot's shoulder tighter, "I shall enter that city, I don't c-"

The four warriors on electric motorcycles shot by, two on either side. The three travelers all watched them speed over the grass and rocks towards Diane and Chaska. For the second time in his life, Dewitt was at a loss of words. Instead he began power-walking back towards the welcoming group. Manuel followed. José yelled after, "You're gonna get yourself killed!"

He stayed put while Dewitt and Manuel approached Diane with such purpose that Chaska's soldiers raised their weapons to stop the two from coming any closer.

"Forget the sins of our acquaintance, because he is nothing but that. Whatever qualms you share with him, you shall not find with me," Dewitt kept his hands up while taking small steps forward, "What you can find is a powerful ally."

"Should I kill him?" Chaska asked Diane out of the corner of his mouth. She shook her head, the turned to the Dutchman, "What could you possibly offer me?"

"Wealth beyond your wildest dreams."

"Cahokia creates its own wealth. You know this, it's why you're here."

"An army of a hundred thousand able bodied men, if you let me tour your markets?"

Diane smugly tittered, "Unnecessary, untrustworthy, and unsustainable."

"Understandable," fired back Dewitt, "An introduction to the highest courts of Europe?"

"Nope."

"Stock in the most powerful company in the world?"

From this, she surmised that he worked for the Dutch East India Company, the first publicly traded corporation in history. It had been so dominant and tyrannical in the last eight decades that the only entity that could keep the VOC in check was the Kingdom of France. Dewitt held a lofty position at a company whose market cap would be worth eight trillion dollars in 2019 when adjusted for inflation.

"VOC stock may be valuable now, but not for long," Diane crossed her arms.

"Is there some news that I should be abreast of? Trouble in Batavia? Look, I appreciate the hostility but all I'm searching for is a symbiotic relationship, not an investment advisor."

Diane's patience ran dry, "Kiyąąh sizíní. It's a saying in Cahokia, it's a little bit hard to translate from the original Navajo. I believe the general jist is 'fuck off' but with violent ends."

Chaska and his soldiers brought out their weapons, rubbing them suggestively. Dewitt chortled and bowed to Diane, before backing away.

"Deion Sanders," Diane realized out loud. Chaska was confused, "What is that?"

"Never mind. Let's make sure that they take off and head east."

"You're going to let them go?"

Diane realized two things: First, she was incredibly interested to see what a teenage could do with a single prop plane in renaissance Europe. Second, Diane felt responsible for José's misfortune and didn't have the heart to kill him.

The plane swung out into a cloudless patch, the eastern seaboard stretching from either end of José's view. Dark clouds from the Atlantic crept towards the shore, promising tumult and rain. Dewitt and Manuel chatted excitedly in the back cabin in Dutch.

"There's really only one way. It will take an international coalition with continued military and resource support from all transnational corporations," Dewitt said, stroking his moustache.

"So, we head for Versailles?"

"After a few necessary rendezvouses. It's paramount that we get out in front of this. Spain is my only worry."

"The bewitched king?"

"Exactly. Carlos' swimmers never seem to reach their goal or even leave their marks. Who really knows who shall win the crown but what's important is that we convince him before he departs."

"But why? Is he not just a French puppet?"

"The Habsburgs' domain is expansive and Carlos' will is under dispute..."

"I see. It shall be war."

Dewitt nodded, "which would completely drain attention from the central objective." He rose and shouted to José in English, "José, my brave soul, remember, north of Boston, you'll spot three large ships sitting in the water."

The three travelers landed on a semi-flat strip of beach just south of the three large mercantile VOC brigantines. Dewitt's men stopped to watch the descent and landing. As Manuel burst out of the plane's doors, the men cheered, pounding the ground with their rifles and swords. Dewitt followed shortly after and the men roared even louder.

José wasn't sure if he should leave the plane, but after a pointed clearing of the throat by Manuel, José stepped out. Dewitt had already made his way over to a group of his mercenaries, all conversing with wild, expressive gestures. Manuel held out his hand to shake and said, "You'll join us, right?"

"What do you mean?"

"Back to Europe, of course. We'll need you. The plane needs you."

Crossing the Atlantic had never occurred to him. "There's not enough fuel to get across."

"We shan't fly, the ship has plenty of room."

José hated the idea of putting the plane on an ancient wooden boat, but he knew he had no real say in the matter. Even though Dewitt and Manuel treated José with more respect than Nicholls, he was still technically a prisoner. They weren't going to let go of the plane and neither was José.

Dewitt's men led their shrewd commander into a small tent, battered by the wind and sea spray. Inside, Anthony Colve sat, nursing a black eye and a broken rib. Colve looked up at Dewitt with intense derision and little surprise, "Dewitt, please tell me you gave Arend a proper Christian burial?"

"I did not, because Arend lives on. He currently resides just outside of Utrecht, however he has resigned from active military duty."

Colve scoffed, tenderly touching his torso. Dewitt plowed ahead, "I've come to give advice, old friend. What were your orders from the Stadholder after the British took New Amsterdam?"

"You are not and have never been a member of the Dutch Military thus I am under no obligation to reveal anything."

"He told you to lay low, to not poke the lion. Obviously, he knows something that you don't. William has designs on England. Yes, his marriage with Mary may solidify it, but now none of it matters. The British, French, Spanish, even the VOC, will forget all of their royal strife. Our greatest foe lies to the West."

Colve and Dewitt had grown up together in the courts of the Oost-indisch Huis, the headquarters for the VOC. In their prepubescent years, they had been rivals, then had become friends during a rousing hunting expedition in Montferrat. After Colve had decided to go the military route and Dewitt had committed to the family business, their relationship became rocky once more, constantly butting heads over the ever-increasing power that the VOC held over the Dutch republic.

"Since when is the VOC responsible for the New World?" Colve spat back. Dewitt yanked Colve up and dragged him out of the tent. They stared at the plane which was being secured down to a large wooden board by a sea of men.

"You still own shares, right?" Dewitt asked. Colve nodded dumbly, trying to convince himself that what he was seeing wasn't an illusion.

"I suggest you build more housing, purchase more weapons, and kiss the asses of the French. Do NOT aggress against the Natives, you'd regret it, at least not until I re-turn. Batten down the hatches for war is coming, one greater than ever before. I have business in Europe, but I shall return here with an army larger than any this world has ever seen."

-

CHAPTER

17

April, 1685

A large metal crane, adorned from the base to the load line with leaves, pinecones, and spiritual totems, lifted a giant metal statue of the fertility god Kokopelli onto a dugout foundation. The revered trickster god clanged down with a boom, followed by a resounding cascade of whoops from the surrounding crowd. Diane and Onawa watched from inside a bisoon, a six wheeled vehicle powered by an array of solar panels covering the bulbous surface. After a few years of development, bisoons were slowly being distributed to high ranking officials and certain industries. They reached a top speed of 400 borels per hour. The cabin of the bisoon was luxurious, covered in a soft cotton material with a spacious trunk.

"Shall we?" Onawa asked, while munching on a handful of peanuts. Diane shifted the bisoon into first gear and they jolted forward. Two more bisoons followed, full of Diane and Onawa's accompanying security team. A large portion of the onlookers turned from Kokopelli to watch the vehicles kick up soil and race south.

Over the last three years, Diane's empire had expanded from the western most tip of the Appalachians all the way to the Pacific. Hundreds of tribes had joined on, tempted by the promise of easier, more productive lives. Per the Cahokian constitution, as each tribe reached a certain population marker, they were given a spot on the Council. On April 5th, 1685, the Council held exactly 498 members. After the hundredth member had joined, Diane activated a clause in the constitution that called for the formation of the High Council, an exclusive group of twenty chiefs deemed suitable representatives for and by the various regional sectors of the Cahokian Empire. The High Council and Diane were the executive and judicial branch, while the Council was the legislative.

Diane and Onawa, who had been voted onto the High Council, were on their way to the southern border of the CE, where the Cahokian army was steadily hacking their way down the continent. The Spanish and their grossly loyal Mayan and Aztec subjects had rejected all peaceful negotiations with the CE after learning that their new neighbors to the north did not share their devotion for *Gold, Glory, and God*. Negotiations with the French had played out similarly, however under the command of the wise Louis the Great, the French had almost completely retreated back across the Atlantic. The Castilians had issued an edict of war against the CE in mid 1683, forcing the High Council's hand. In October of 1683, the Cahokian military began its march towards Central America, slaughtering Spaniards and Mesoamericans. Diane had convinced the High Council and the Council to try to persuade the indigenous Mayans and Aztecs to abandon their oppressive conquistadors but few had. The Catholic hegemony had taken root almost two centuries before Diane's arrival, and in this instance, faith was thicker than technology. But not stronger.

One side was armed with automatic weapons, bulletproof armor, tanks, motorcycles, grenades, missiles, laughing gas, night vision goggles, snipers, long distance radios, canvas tents, packaged rations, and fully prepared medical backup. The other side fought with single-load pistols, clubs, sticks, spears, swords, arrows, and the occasional trained wolf. Needless to say, the Cahokians had pushed the Spaniards down to modern day Panama, a geographical bottleneck that trapped the Habsburgian empire in South America. The only other colonial force that remained in North America was the British, who, after witnessing Cahokia's conquest of New Spain and New France, quickly established tenuous trading routes with their emergent neighbors.

"We need to discuss the Cochimi," Onawa mentioned forcefully. Diane huffed, swerving to avoid a boulder,

"There's been nothing in the last few weeks, but I agree. We can visit them on the way back."

"Sooner rather than later."

Onawa was referring to the Cochimi, a rogue tribe that occupied what would have been called the Baja California Peninsula. After making contact with the CE, Cochimi had welcomed the technological advancements for at least a year and then cut off all communication with the rest of the empire. For the last few months, reports of Cochimi raids on neighboring tribes plagued the High Council and Diane to no end.

"We'll stop there on the way back north," reassured Diane.

Onawa wasn't going to let up, "Often the destruction of a minority can save the majority. We should send in the Monsters."

"The Monsters are not ready. I'm- We're not going to make this into some tyrannical totalitarian military state! Negotiations come first, always!"

"What haven't we tried?"

"I have people all over the continent gathering intel for me. Patience, Onawa. Tell me, what's going on in the Northwest? I hear rumors about overfishing?"

"The Duwamish," Onawa conceded.

"We can't have people using electricity in the water! You know how dangerous that is?"

"I'm not sure why you're yelling at me..."

Diane sagged, her anger receded, "You're my High Council totem right now. I meant nothing." She pressed a large square button in the center of the dashboard. A blurt of static from the bisoon's speakers crackled, followed by a muffled "Yes, ma'am?"

"Radio message for the CCC, to the Du-" Diane glanced at Onawa questioningly.

"Duwamish."

Diane continued, "to the Duwamish from my private line. Got it?"

"Ready when you are."

Diane cleared her throat, "Overfishing is a serious crime, which can result in a serious penalty. If I continue to receive reports of depleted reserves of marine life, the High Council will impose several strict embargos on the Duwamish. Over."

"Copy!"

Onawa twiddled with her grey hair, waited for Diane's breathing to return to normal, and asked, "When's the last time you had sex?"

Diane swerved the bisoon to the right to avoid an unfortunate saguaro cactus, who caught the brunt of the bisoon's side view mirror. Onawa grabbed the door as Diane corrected their path. The convoy behind them flashed their headlights in concern. Diane flashed back that they were fine. Onawa puckered her lips, "Have you had sex since you've come here?"

"This is not appropriate."

"So, our relationship ends at colleagues?"

Diane tightened her hands on the wheel, her knuckles turning white, "I'm too busy."

"Oh, come now, all you need is a couple of braves and some salvia-"

"Onawa!"

"Do you like women? I often thought you and Nikan were very close."

"I don't want to talk about this."

"Interesting," Onawa began braiding her own hair, "Do they not copulate where you come from?"

"Of course, they do."

"And you?"

"It never appealed to me."

Onawa saw her opportunity and took it, "What about Chaska?"

"He..."

Diane and Onawa's front right tire launched in the air in a flurry of flame and dirt, flipping their bisoon. The giant metal beast's forward momentum carried it through an entire loop and it landed on all six wheels before veering off into a ditch. Diane's last thought was *landmine*. The other two bisoons skidded to a stop on either side and soldiers hopped out.

Gunfire erupted from all sides, so the soldiers covered themselves behind the bisoons, loading their weapons. The Cochimi had found them.

The last three years had been a whirlwind of dukedoms and monarchies, most of which José had never heard about. As the foremost expert on fuel-powered engines, José moved around Europe to show off the plane, under

Dewitt's command. The main objective was to raise funding for the production of more engines, however Dewitt also intended it to be a large-scale recruitment for his American crusade. The Dutch tycoon had been spending a lot of time schmoozing generals.

In April, 1685, José's traveling troupe found themselves in Florence, the dying ember of a once great cultural mecca. The capital of the Grand Duchy of Tuscany had suffered through a bout of bubonic plague just forty years prior and a flubbing by the once-powerful Medici family. José learned all of this by listening to Piero, a filthy, shaggy slave boy with an encyclopedic knowledge of Western European aristocracy and Tuscan brothels. The former was quite informative, but José kept Piero around for the latter.

Sitting together on a comfy sofa, Piero assailed José in Italian, "It's really quite pleasant what they do in Prato, I would never have thought that the back of your knee was such a sensitive erogenous zone. I must show you." Piero reached for José's legs, but quickly retracted after receiving a vicious slap.

José replied in Spanish with a great deal of Italian words, "I'm no longer interested in *how* you know so much about brothels, but *why*?"

"Master, they cut off my balls, not my knees."

"I'm going to cut off your knees if you don't let me focus."

"Deepest apologies, master." Piero bowed his head so reverently it became sarcastic. In front of them, from wall to wall, a line of prostitutes waited for the pilot's decision.

José surveyed the girls carefully, twiddling with an opium pipe in his right hand. After losing his trusty THC wax pen, José had pined for another manner of escaping the existential dread that came with sobriety. After the VOC ships had arrived in Amsterdam, José discovered that the small quantities of marijuana he could find were disappointingly impotent. Manuel had shown him how to smoke the black liquid which sufficiently scratched José's itch and then some.

José wagged his finger at Dona Chiara, the madam of the esteemed establishment, a large goose-necked woman who scurried over to kneel by José's side.

"Signore?"

"Could I have three?"

"It will be three times the regular, of course."

"It's not my bill. I'll take the two brunettes on the left and the girl in the green thingy, dress, whatever it's called..."

"Corset. Right away, signore!" Dona Chiara stood and clapped her hands. The girls dispersed quickly, while Dona Chiara ushered José's selections up the stairs. José and Piero sprang to their feet.

"Not after what you did in Arezzo," José pushed Piero back onto the sofa sternly. Piero frowned while José ascended the brothel's steps.

In the private bedroom, at the sight of three brunette girls sitting patiently on the bed, José began stripping off his clothes before Dona Chiara had a chance to close the door. "What are your names?" He asked hurriedly.

"Antonella," said the brunette sitting closest to him.

"Antonella, as well."

"Me too."

Jose cocked his head, "You're all named Antonella?"

"Think of us as a single woman, yearning to pleasure you in several different ways at once," purred another, this Antonella with shorter curly hair. José couldn't argue with that, so he stripped off his briefs. The third Antonella stood as the other two worked quickly to untie her corset. It fell to the ground and José gulped. Large breasts spilling over an hourglass shape. José's gaze meandered up to her smirking face. She approached José, grabbed his now attentive Joséito, and whispered in his ear, "My name isn't actually Antonella."

"....."

"It's just a trick to get young men out of their own heads. As well as get other things out of their heads." Her arm started moving. The two other girls reclined back on the bed. Faux-Antonella sped up gradually, "What do you want me to say?"

"Huh?" José's eyes started rolling upwards and he found it difficult to concentrate on speech. She asked again and he managed, "That you were wrong about kissing Kyle Peterson!"

"Who's Kyle Peterson?"

"Fuck Kyle Peterson!"

José grabbed a bedpost to steady himself as she moved her hand faster, "You want to fuck Kyle Peterson?"

"No! No! I want to kill him! I want you to say that you want to kill him!"

Faux-Antonella bit her lip and cried seductively, "José, let's murder Kyle Peterson, once and for all!"

The two Antonellas giggled from the bed as José collapsed onto the bed, gasping for breath. José grabbed for opium pipe just as post-coital clarity threatened to rear its existential head.

"Who was she?" José's eyes fluttered open to find Faux-Antonella propped up on one arm, emerald eyes twinkling.

"Only after you tell me your real name," he replied.

"Like you'll remember it. Noemi," the girl said playfully. She spoke almost perfect Castilian with a Tuscan accent, her pronunciation and cadence sounded like river water on a crisp spring day. The other two girls had dozed off into poppy-hazes.

"How long have you been...doing this?"

"I worked my way up. Started in my village and eventually found myself here, in Florence. It's been a long eleven years."

"How old are you?"

Noemi traced a finger down José's leg, "You ask too many questions."

"Fair enough, I'd much rather have one of your interrogations..."

"A score and seven."

José did some quick mental math and squinted, "So you started when you were sixteen?!"

Noemi winked, "Does that excite you?"

"Not at all. That's outright predatory."

Noemi shrugged lazily, "Where do you come from?"

José's mouth hung open as he tried to formulate an answer, but a knock at the door saved him, "For the love of god, Piero! Go away!"

Manuel, dressed in a traditional Iberic tunic, hair in braids down to his shoulders, stepped in. José quickly covered himself while Noemi made no effort at all, turning to face Manuel with a smile. Manuel glared at José, "You're a fucking slippery one. Still not as slippery as that little tyke you call a servant. He's causing a raucous, peeping in on all these nice ladies, flashing his cauterized manhood at them like some sort of paradoxical freak."

"Shit," José agreed absentmindedly as he sprang from the bed and began throwing on his clothes. Noemi handed him his shirt, "You never answered my question?"

"What question?" José buttoned up his shirt, while Manuel tapped his foot impatiently.

"Who was she? The girl that you lost to Kyle Peterson?"

"Nobody. She's not important to me anymore."

Manuel grabbed him and dragged him out.

"Piero! Piero! We're leaving, you fucking degenerate!" José yelled as Manuel and him stormed through the building. The sounds of ceramics smashing and high-pitched screams echoed from somewhere deep in the confines of massive bordello. Piero came running, sans pants.

"Gods forgive him," growled Manuel, then to José, "Boss is furious, we've been searching for you for hours. I believe Vincenzo has had a breakthrough."

Vincenzo was a Tuscan mathematician who had been hired by Dewitt to help José develop new technologies using the airplane's engine. José disliked Vincenzo due to the polymath's irritating habit of speaking condescendingly. Vincenzo despised José due to the foreigner's lack of knowledge on the physical and mathematical nature of how the plane and its engine worked. Nonetheless, José was the sole expert on the plane's innards, so Vincenzo played nice as long as the gold flowed, and José played nice as long as the VOC paid for his opium and visits to the whorehouse.

José, Manuel, and Piero reached the private villa on the bluffs of the Due Strade, an outskirt of Florence, where Dewitt had housed their operation. It was a formidable estate, covered in ivy, and red brick. Fountains, renaissance paintings and sculptures, antiquated war equipment, large torches, and Vincenzo's mathematical chalk formulas adorned the walls. Dewitt wanted ideas to flow through the minds of the villa's residents, so he gave Vincenzo and José full permission to trash the property for the good of innovative spontaneity.

The three climbed through the vast hallways, reaching the top floor where Vincenzo's penthouse looked out over glimmering Florence. Dewitt was bent over a large stone table covered in papers, metal gadgets, and writing utensils.

Vincenzo, a broad faced, pale man with a hook nose, leaned on the balcony railing, gesticulating wildly and attempting to explain his idea to Dewitt, "The stern would allow more control over navigation, and without the weight of the sail-"

The Tuscan paused when José, Manuel, and Piero entered the terrace. Dewitt shooed Piero with his hand like a stray. Piero saluted and departed.

"How good of you to join us, comrade," Dewitt shot daggers at José, "Signore Viviani has an idea on how to get our army across the Atlantic."

Vincenzo muttered in the Tuscan dialect something about having to get advice from a degenerate sex-crazed opium addict and moved towards the table. He extracted the large sheet that Dewitt had been revising, holding it out to José. When José reached for it, Vincenzo pulled it back and asked venomously, "Are your hands clean?"

"Nope, they're covered in the fluids of your aunt."

The mathematician went red.

"Vincenzo..." Dewitt was constantly mediating their tiffs. The Tuscan handed the sheet over to José who theatrically pretended to hold the paper like it would fall apart at any second. Vincenzo faced his ire towards the view of the city. José ran his eyes over the sheet, sticking his tongue out of the corner of his mouth pensively.

"This would be aquatic?"

Vincenzo turned around and confirmed by blinking once. José pointed to a corner of the sheet, "This part, what material would you store the engine in?"

"Wood, of course."

"The engine's vibrations will destroy the hull before you make it out of the harbor."

"Metal then." Vincenzo hated being at the mercy of José's counsel. The young man was milking every second. José was thinking about the summers of his youth when Bernie's family would take him up to their lake house in southern Wisconsin. Their rickety boat would only give them a couple of days of wake surfing before the weak little engine would inevitably break down. After an hour of watching Steve, Bernie's stepfather, struggle with the engine, José and Bernie would sneak off to smoke spliffs in the parking lot of a nearby Jewel Osco. Then, stoned, they would enter the store and buy the entire candy section. After a campfire, Bernie would fall asleep to a movie and José would try to make pitifully moves on Candace, Bernie's much older and very uninterested sister.

"José?" Dewitt's exasperation pulled him out of his futuristic nostalgia.

"Plastic. You need to cover the engine in plastic."

Vincenzo made finger purses and cried, "What in God's good name is *plastic*?"

-

April, 1685

"Onawa...Onawa..." mumbled Diane deliriously. The old woman's face rested on the dash, blood pooling onto her sandaled feet. The spatter of gun fire outside reminded Diane of their situation. She tried to unbuckle her seat belt with her right arm but it wasn't responding, so Diane tried her left arm. She could feel her left arm, and almost fainted again as she saw her broken radius sticking out. Gritting her teeth, Diane unfastened, scooted over to Onawa, slowly lifted her friend's head up, then quickly dropped it back to the dash, gagging.

One of Diane's private security men, Jeruk, slammed up against the window of the bisoon, waving frantically for Diane to get down or let him enter, she wasn't sure. Before Jeruk could clarify, a bullet sliced through his temples and he fell limp against the glass. A few more yells and gunfire, then only the sound of triumphant whooping. She held her breath and once more lifted Onawa's corpse off the dash to open the glove compartment. Inside an automatic pistol lay there, pristine, ready to fire. Diane shuddered as she put her weight against Onawa's pulp in order to extract the carton of bullets.

After kicking open the door, Diane tumbled out of the bisoon, pistol cocked, but found that her legs were equally as useless as her right arm. A scratchy voice tsked and said in accented Sauk, "The Unforsaken One told of something falling into our laps today."

Unforsaken One? Diane thought with her face in the blood and oil-soaked sand. Several pairs of calloused hands grabbed and rolled her onto her back, one snatching away the pistol. As her eyes adjusted, the voice spoke once more, coming from a svelte Cochimi warrior, "The Unforsaken One's power is great, greater than any person or thing in Cahokia."

Diane laughed deliriously.

"His soul binds us together," the figure swayed back and forth in a fever. Diane's vision cleared and she was surprised at her captor's puerile face. He couldn't have been a few years older than José, but this young man's face was arrogant, framed by a necklace of rotting human fingers.

Five minutes later, the Cochimi zealots had bound Diane's limbs together tightly and set fire to her wrecked bisoon. They had commandeered the other two bisoons, throwing Diane in the back of one and loading Onawa's and the security team's bodies into the other. She watched as the rest of the troop hopped on motorbikes. A droopy woman climbed into the driver's seat of the bisoon, starting the engine, as the boy with the gruesome necklace entered the spacious trunk with Diane. They hadn't gagged her so Diane said carefully, "All of Cahokia will be searching for me. I have a scheduled ETA and I've been communicating with home base which has the general location of our last broadcast, minutes before your ambush."

The boy grinned, showing at least four yellow teeth.

Their bisoon lurched forward as the Cochimi posse moved Southwest. Climbing onto Diane, the boy began fondling her, "Let me show you his power."

Diane tried to fight off his advances so he tightened her bonds until the twine cut into her skin. The boy began stripping off Diane's clothes in a hungry trance. Diane screamed as her protruding radial bone scraped against the floor.

After several hours, Diane curled up in the back of bisoon, bruised and violated, wanting to die. The boy was sitting on the side in the passenger's seat, chattering happily in Cochimi to the driver who just lamely nodded along while focusing on the road.

The bisoon screeched to a halt, pitching Diane forward so her face hit the back of the driver's seat. Blood poured from her nose down the side of her face. The back of the bisoon was opened and several pairs of hands dragged her out. Her bonds were cut by two gnarly large men who clenched down on either of her biceps, squeezing them so hard Diane wished they would return the twine. With little effort, the two burly Cochimi lifted Diane a few inches off the ground and carried her through the camp.

Hammocks and storage bags hung off every palm tree, through which Diane could see clear blue water lapping onto a pristine white sand beach. Hundreds of Cochimi men, women, and children milled around large huts made of brick and corrugated steel. Despite the massive amount of coagulated blood in her nose, the smell of rotting flesh filled Diane with a sense of dread. She spotted several men hunched around a bonfire, spit roasting a shapely human leg.

The two men carrying Diane sped towards a towering building that was located on higher ground slightly inland. Colored glass covered every inch of the outside walls so that it was almost impossible to look at without being blinded by a myriad of reflections. As they neared, Diane noticed a man-made moat surrounding the glimmering temple. A dozen vaquita porpoises floated glumly in the murky water. Diane watched three small girls dump a bucket of human parts into the moat and the vaquitas came to life, fighting violently over the scraps.

A large mechanical hum announced the lowering drawbridge, a thick slab of steel-reinforced wood which clanged down a few feet in front of Diane and her chaperones. The men hurled her onto the drawbridge. She collapsed a few feet near the edge, moaning from the countless splinters that had just entered her from the unfinished wood. She looked back at the two Cochimi who stood steadfast at the foot of the drawbridge and the message was clear. She was meant to cross into the temple.

Diane shakily propped herself up on one hand, tried to push herself up onto two feet, but found that her legs were still unresponsive.

The man on the left whistled sharply. Diane felt the drawbridge begin to rise up. She quickly positioned herself so her feet were pointed towards the open entrance so she wouldn't slide down on her head. Once the wooden slab reached a steep enough angle, Diane tumbled, receiving several more splinters on the way down. The drawbridge slammed shut and Diane found herself in utter darkness.

"Welcome Cahokian," croaked a synthesized voice that seemed to emanate from all around. Lights in all different colors appeared, running up and illuminating the exterior. A sea of angular chandeliers hung from the high ceiling, all switching through the color spectrum in a melodic rhythm. If Diane hadn't been dragged to an annual Christmas light show or had never used YouTube before, she would have been mesmerized. She lowered her gaze to find an odd-looking creature inspecting her from a raised platform in the center of the room. The creature, a completely black nylon body covered with string-lights and glowing slanted wolf eyes that changed color, crouched in a feral pose.

"You made all this?" Diane questioned from the floor. The creature pulled up slightly, then boomed in its robotic voice, "I'm Zula, the Unforsaken One, and you are mortal! Kneel before me before I smite you!"

"I like the electrical work," Diane said absentmindedly. Zula roared, sending waves of color up to the top.

"Damn, you even got the voice synchronization!"

"You fool, it is time for me to eat your soul!"

"I'd hire you on as an engineer, but we have a strict no cannibalism policy."

"Silence! Cochimi is my earthly domain, and once I reach my true form, the entire world will shudder under my mighty footsteps!"

"How big is your true form?"

"Mightier than the tallest redwood, stronger than the fiercest storm! The Cochimi will ravage my enemies until none but us are left..."

Zula stalked across the platform, expecting the usual reaction of subservient terror. Diane would have been amused if she wasn't so gruesomely injured. Zula pressed a secret button on the floor with a sparkling foot, causing the audio distortion to skyrocket, "Now I shall feed off your soul!"

"Look, I know you're not a spirit. You're a sick cannibal with a knack for electrical engineering."

Zula stood still, unaccustomed to being challenged. A few moments of silence passed before the creature began pacing again, then said, "I would not expect a mortal to understand. You're at death's door. It would be wise to appeal to me."

Diane sighed. She cracked her neck and placed her index finger behind her right ear. Roughly two years ago, Diane had installed a transmitter chip just under the skin which would submit a long-distance broadcast to the nearest Cahokian receiver. After a few seconds the transmitting signal found a receiver and a gruff but familiar voice answered, "Diane? This is the emergency line…"

Diane held back tears of joy. Of all the Cahokians who could have answered her call, Hatha had. He was a gregarious man who assisted Chaska in many of his campaigns against the Spanish. He was as flamboyant as he was skilled in military strategy, but Diane got along with him because Hatha spoke English. The Comanche general had spent many years trading with the English, so many nights, exhausted from spending all day stumbling through the Sauk language, Diane would find her way to Hatha's tent with a bottle of fermented sap and the two would shoot the breeze. It also presented a perfect opportunity for Diane to deceive Zula. Diane raised her one good arm and said ominously in English, "I've been captured by the Cochimi. They're cannibals. I'm badly injured but secure inside a large reflective building. I'm requesting a protocol 845 on all surrounding areas, save for my secure location."

"Diane…" buzzed Hatha, concerned, "Are you sure?"

Zula shrank, trying to understand the foreign babble. Diane continued, staring directly into the Cochimi spirit's eyes, "It's an opportunity to demonstrate the Monsters."

The line was quiet for an unbearable moment. "Don't leave your location."

Still with eyes locked onto Zula, Diane slumped a little, as if her *spell* had taken some effort. Really, she was losing blood.

The Unforsaken One stepped down the platform, hissing with satisfaction. "Your incantations mean nothing, witch. Prepare to have the flesh ripped off of you."

"Squadron inbound in 30 seconds," Hatha buzzed in Diane's ear. Zula produced a long, curved blade and approached Diane, the synthesized audio of lips being wetted bounced around like hundreds of electric eels slithering over each other.

"I'll give one last chance to surrender," Diane offered in Sauk, scooting away from the approaching cannibal.

"Northerners always taste worse, it must be your diet. Still, you taste sweeter than a Spaniard." Zula leaned down, wafting an extremely foul stench that could only be formed by not bathing for months. Diane retched. The Unforsaken One inserted the knife into Diane's left arm where her bone stuck out. Diane almost fainted. Zula flicked the tip out, taking a chuck of skin with it, then swallowed the piece whole. "Not bad."

Hatha tuned in, "Incoming! Hold on to something!"

In Sauk, Diane stated calmly, "There's no such thing as witches or spirits. You know this, I'm sure you do. But, you just tried to eat a god."

The ground began to rumble. Deafening booms knocked down light strips, tiles, and chandeliers from the walls and ceiling. Zula's knife fell to the floor, the Unforsaken One watched the shimmering temple quake.

"Those, my sparkly little fraud, are my monsters and they are not happy with you."

⊕

"It's set with heat or cold?" inquired Vincenzo, who, for the first time, was genuinely interested in what José had to say. Manuel, Dewitt, and him all wanted to hear more about this magical substance that was lighter than metal yet more moldable. José was having a hard time explaining something so ubiquitous in his own world, "Half of the plane is made of plastic! Why is this only coming up now?"

Vincenzo sheepishly shuffled through the papers, "I was instructed to focus on the engine, not the composition of materials."

"No, no," Dewitt wagged his finger at the Tuscan, "You cannot blame financing for this. My directions were broad. This is beside the point, where can we obtain plastic?"

"I think we have to make it," José said, but had no idea how to go about doing so.

Dewitt plopped down on a stool and poured himself a glass of wine from one of the several bottles on the table, "Are there samples of this plastic material on the plane?"

José nodded. Dewitt gulped down the glass and refilled haphazardly, while saying decisively, "Vincenzo will remain here and try his best to reproduce plastic with any and all information which José will give him in verbal and written form. You two have this morning, and only this morning, as matters in France require José's presence, so you both shall stay here until you share an equivalent knowledge of plastics. Then, Vincenzo will be given samples of this plastic from the flying machine, anything that can be spared. José, see you on the runway in a few hours."

Dewitt downed the wine, chucked the glass off the balcony, and stormed out, Manuel following in his wake. Vincenzo pulled on his kinky Mediterranean hair, avoiding eye contact with José, who had lit an ornate bamboo opium pipe and was in the process of making himself comfortable on a plush chair.

"I have a sinking feeling that you have nothing else to add," Vincenzo said, brandishing a quill and paper. Grey smoke poured out of the sides of José's mouth as he melted into the cushions. He mumbled, "Tell me about Galileo."

Vincenzo's late mentor had been the famous polymath, Galileo, which tickled José. Vincenzo poured himself a glass of wine, silently assured himself that there would be other projects after this, and resigned to humoring José.

"He was a quack."

"Why?" replied José, puffing the opium harder. Vincenzo flopped down in a chair facing José and inquired suspiciously, "Why are you so interested in him? Most considered him a heretic."

"How so?"

"Well, until his house arrest, he fought tooth and nail for his theory of heliocentrism, the idea that earth and other planets revolve around the sun, not vice-versa."

"No shit!" Some seventeenth century beliefs never ceased to amuse José. Vincenzo cocked his brow, shocked that José took to the revolutionary theory so quickly, "Be careful what you say, the Pope's ears are everywhere."

"Where I come from, Galileo is very famous."

"Really? But how? He died but two score years ago and all of his work is suppressed by the church?"

José put down the opium pipe and his eyes fluttered closed for a few seconds. Vincenzo's knee bounced impatiently until José slowly materialized back, "Not sure, Vinny, guess my people don't bend to the church as much."

"Where are you from exactly?"

"I'm from out west."

"Cahokia?" Vincenzo leaned in, eyes blazing with curiosity.

"Fuck that place. You couldn't pay me to say I'm from there."

"You know them well? Is your land at war with the Cahokians?"

For months now, every European could talk of nothing else but the astoundingly powerful civilization that had been discovered in the New World. The French, the economic and militaristic powerhouse of Europe had fled the Western continent with their tails tucked, and Spain's impending defeat was the central topic of conversation for vagabonds and aristocrats alike. All other political news became trivial. The rising anti-Catholic sentiments in England manifested in the Monmouth Rebellion, the future of the Habsburg line, and the bombardment of Genoa fell by the way side. Even the Venetian crusade against the fearsome Ottomans stopped being a pressing issue. Everybody wanted to know more about the futuristic foes that had managed to enter the world stage so suddenly and with great success. Rumors of fantastical technology and metallic beasts echoed in the courts and plagued all established hegemonies, all of which, at first, voiced passionate but ironic skepticism. José's tour of the plane had shut almost all of the non-believers up, with more and more spiritual leaders joining Dewitt's plight against Cahokia. The VOC director had so far done a splendid job of tempting the capitalists with promises of riches beyond their wildest dreams and sympathizing with the churches to drum up support for a holy crusade.

José and company left out the fact that the only plane they had was on death's door. Whale oil was too viscous and its combustion point was too high. José flew the plane now only once every two months. Each time the motor sounded worse. Dewitt was aware but swore José and Manuel to secrecy.

"My country doesn't exist. The leader of Cahokia took my land, my family, my world away from me. It needs to be burned to the ground." José grew dark and foreboding, staring at Vincenzo with intense sincerity.

"Who is their leader?"

José shook his head. Vincenzo frowned but moved on, "Are the tales of Cahokia true?"

"How did Galileo's cock taste in your mouth?"

Vincenzo sipped his wine. For the first time, he saw the grumbling ne'er-do-well in a different light, troubled by war and genocide.

"Galileo and I had just adjourned a seminar and decided to take a stroll through the Cathedral of Pisa. Galileo couldn't stop talking about Fibonacci, and I couldn't stop talking about the nasty bout of syphilis my sister had just died from. This is how most of the conversations went, you see, us shouting different subjects at each other, hoping the other would hear enough of the other's. We were passing underneath a large bronze chandelier that was swinging to and fro. Galileo fell silent and halted, drool began to cascade from his bottom lip, just watching the decoration swing over and over. I kept on talking about my late sister, god rest her soul, when he shouted "Eureka!" and ran to the nearest quill and paper. I pursued the madman, demanding to know what the fuss was. After catching his breath, for he was not a fit man, he exclaimed that he had just discovered a *pendulum*, something he said would unlock the secrets of the universe. I rebuffed his theory as a bout of hysteria, not understanding how a rusty chandelier could reveal the secrets of the six planets of our solar system and beyond, but-"

"There's more than six planets in our solar system," José carelessly interrupted. Vincenzo, furious that his charming anecdote was interrupted by a correction, exclaimed, "How many are there then?"

"Nine! Mercury, Venus, Earth, Mars, Jupiter, Saturn, Uranus, Neptune, and Pluto."

"You can't just name Roman gods!"

"Well, now technically, there are only eight."

Vincenzo sprang up in mock surprise, "There were nine, now there are eight! Tomorrow you'll be telling me of Vulcan, the twelfth planet! The two suns, wait no, now there are three!"

A grin slowly formed on José's face, then he stood and sauntered out. The seething Tuscan mathematician hovered by the table, then began doing the only thing that felt somewhat appropriate - chugging the rest of the wine.

José made his way out of the estate and up into the mountains, towards a freshly constructed runway. Dewitt and Manuel were already there, directing a crew of Dewitt's personal mercenaries that were in the refined process of loading up the plane with cargo and fuel. These men came mostly from Bavaria and France, but all had somehow fallen into debt, which was how Dewitt bound them to secrecy. Furthermore, every man who worked near the plane unfortuitously disappeared or became permanently incapacitated by smallpox. The poor souls were doomed the minute they fell into trouble with the VOC.

Manuel ushered José towards the nose of the plane, where Dewitt was leaning over a hand drawn map of Europe. The wiry Dutchman pointed his bony index finger at extremely unrealistic depiction of western Europe. José never enjoyed geography but the unmistakable inaccuracy of the map made José snortle. Dewitt ignored him, "Versailles. A few miles outside of Paris."

"Why is England so goddamn large? I'm pretty sure Scandinavia is not an island, either."

Dewitt rolled up the map and faced his insolent pilot, "We're going to the zenith, every major monarch from the House of Bourbon and Habsburg will be in attendance. They know of the flying machine's existence but have yet to see it for themselves. This is our chance to show them what lies to the West. Do you want revenge on Cahokia?"

José nodded. Dewitt smashed the map into José's chest, then stalked off to yell at a clumsy Bavarian man trying to lift a fuel barrel by himself.

Manuel nudged José gently in the shoulder, "He just despises royalty. They're the only people that he has to bow to. Focus on not making us look like fools."

"Thanks, Manu, that makes me feel a lot better," José replied with an eye roll. A faint yodel made them look towards the edge of the runway where a small figure came sprinting towards the plane. Trained guards began firing their muskets at the intruder who began zigzagging nimbly without slowing. José shouted for a ceasefire a few seconds later when he realized it was Piero. The pipsqueak sidled up to José and Manuel, unperturbed from his scrape with death, "You almost forgot me, master!"

"Absolutely not," declared Manuel, throwing his hands gruffly on the struggling Tuscan slave boy, "You're staying here on the ground or in the ground." The muscular Angolan easily pushed Piero to the ground, who got up nonplussed and faced his stringy master. José knelt down to Piero's level and spoke sincerely, "You've got some issues, Piero. Serious issues, some weird stuff that's pretty concerning especially for somebody your age and...situation. I didn't even think eunuchs could be- never mind. I'll be back but, in the meantime, I need you to look after Noemi."

"Who?"

"The girl I was with...the working girl. Green eyes."

"There were three, master."

José glanced up at Manuel, who grinned and shook his head to say that he wasn't going to give them privacy, so José went on, "The girl that was asking me questions while she..."

"She will be more secure than a Sephardic bank!"

While they embraced, José said quietly so Manuel could not overhear, "I will return as soon as I can, with the plane, and you and Noemi will come with me to my homeland."

The flight from Florence to Versailles was uneventful, beyond Dewitt neurotically quizzing José on what to say and how to act with European royalty. His shrill voice and anxious demands put José on edge. He'd never not seen Dewitt calm and collected. At one point during the second half of the journey, Manuel took the yoke as José grumpily changed into a complex three-piece suit. It was black and white, which, when compared with Dewitt and Manuel's colorful tunics, made José look like an expensive sky chauffeur.

Soon the green sharp angles of France's highest court came into view and José directed his descent to a path of even gravel just to the side of the palace grounds.

"Land on the water," commanded Dewitt, pointing to a lengthy pond. José disagreed immediately, "I'm not risking that."

"You must. Look, you can see that they have gathered along the canal."

"We could crash!"

"Appearance, José, is everything to these people. Land on the canal, I give you my word that it is smooth enough."

José craned his neck to see a shockingly large group of people milling around the edge of the canal. He grumbled quietly but redirected his path so he could loop around and land down the length of the mile long canal.

"Those by the water will get wet."

Dewitt grinned mischievously, "That's exactly how we want them."

The plane dipped down, skimming the surface of the placid, moldy water. José tried to spot any imperfections on the bottom while guessing how deep the pond actually was. Crowds of people fled from the sides as the plane dipped farther into the tepid water, spraying it to either side.

Thankfully, the bottom of the pond was relatively smooth so José was able to pull the plane to a stop a few yards from the end. The crowd was regrouping around the edge of the pond, few jeering at the fantastical flying machine, while most clapped and clamored back towards the edge to get a glimpse of the celebrity passengers. Dewitt surprised José by saying, "You first."

"Why me? They don't know who I am."

"Exactly. They just witnessed a historical event and if old Van Oldenbarnevelt appears first, it'll only subtract from the panache."

"What should I say? And in what language?"

"Don't say anything. Just smile, bow once, and stand next to the flyer valiantly. Oh good, they're putting out a walkway."

Some servants had begun placing wooden boards from the pond's edge up to just below the nose of the plane. José scowled, "They have no idea where the door is."

"Open the door but do not show yourself," instructed Dewitt, so José opened the door a crack, causing a wave of exhilaration to run through the crowd. The servants quickly moved the boards to the edge of the door then scurried away.

On the Dutchman's nod, José pushed into the open, stepped down onto the rickety board and gave a deep bow. A hush ran through the crowd. Seconds later, Manuel stepped down, bowing respectfully and confidently. The people grew even quieter. The last two people they expected to exit this mythical flying machine were two non-whites. Finally, after an excruciatingly long minute, Dewitt dropped onto the boards with a thud, raising both arms high in the sky. José couldn't help but be reminded of Nicholls showing off the plane to the New Yorkers. These Europeans had a much different reaction - they exploded into applause, waving of embroidered handkerchiefs, shouting *encore!* and *bravo!*

Dewitt waved, placed his feet shoulder-width apart, and pontificated in French, "Nigh! Nigh is the dawn of a new age! God hath seen fit for us to take to the heavens, travel among his land, fraternize with angels, and spread his word to the ends of the Earth. To my left, stands a prophet, sent by the lord himself to deliver us the means of this wonder of natural philosophy. He hath brought a great flying beast, *a plane* as his people call it. We shall allow a select few to ride with us into God's kingdom, but beware! She's a magnificent, marvelous, mighty, meritorious mount, yet bucks through the air like a rowdy colt at unfathomable speeds. All your questions shall be answered by my crew and I in due time."

Dewitt paused, scanned the crowd, found his target, and knelt. Manuel and José followed suit. "Before anything else, I wish to throw myself at the mercy of the crown and the House of France. I beg your majesty's forgiveness for disrupting the day's events and any possible trauma that I may have caused his subjects or property." Dewitt bowed his head respectfully and all eyes turned to a rather plump, tall man with a pencil thin moustache.

"There are few protestants that I would enjoy watching arrive in my hallowed grounds. Especially one that ridicules so publicly the way my economists run my sovereignty," said the man in a deep booming voice, "Rise and receive thy punishment."

José noticed Dewitt's fists clench as they rose. The crowd waited with baited breath as Louis the Great, the Sun King, pulled at his unimpressive moustache with two pale fingers, then declared, "For the crime of disturbing my polo game, you shall take me on a ride of the heavens so I may look upon the glory of France!"

The onlookers exploded into a patriotic fervor. Men stomped the ground and pounded their hands together, praising Louis and France. Women clapped furiously and waved frilly doilies in the air. This lasted for a good ten minutes, during which José, Manuel, and Dewitt stood in the same place, the pond's murky water soaking into their shoes. Louis adjusted his golden belt, satisfied with the reaction, "Come, kiss my hand, you mercantile buffoon!"

For José, the next several hours were a blur of countless nobles who all had confusingly similar names, wretched senses of humor, unbridled racist ideologies, and immaculate appearances that failed to hide obscene body odors. Dewitt and Manuel stood guard by him, fielding the harder questions about faith and Cahokia, while José explained over and over about how the plane worked. They worked their way through the crowd until Dewitt pulled José aside and whispered, "We are about to be in the presence of the second most important person in the continent. Forewarning, he's not pleasant to look at or to talk to, but for the love of god, maintain formality."

The endless sea of nobility parted and an entourage of finely adorned maids pushed forward a heavy cushioned wheelchair on which sat a startlingly disfigured, inbred human. His legs were either nonexistent or hidden in a mound of cloth from which a twisted body protruded up to a freakishly lopsided, triangular head. Wisps of hair indicated balding, but the prepubescent face made José unsure whether this person was seventeen or seventy. An uneven overbite hung under vacant eyes that stared forward at nothing. This was Charles the Second of Spain.

The Bewitched Spanish King, the last of the Habsburg line, never stood a chance, or from his wheelchair. His father was Philip the Fourth of Spain and his mother was Mariana of Austria. Already inadvisably inbred themselves,

Philip and Mariana, uncle and niece, had gotten married. Charles was the straw that broke the genetic camel's back. Spain had fallen into economic ruin during his reign and the ever-growing threat of Cahokians demolishing their colonies out west had only taken a greater toll on the Spanish monarchy.

The maids halted the wheelchair in front of the newcomers and the pathetic homunculus began to slur laboriously, "Welcome, thee...I only wish...to soar upon...upon...the cloud..."

The rest of his speech was indiscernible but from the reactions of the crowd and Dewitt, José understood that Charles was thrilled. Dewitt knelt in front of the king and gingerly kissed his hand, gesturing after for José to do the same. The king smelled even worse than the others and José almost fainted in the royal lap but was able to fend off lightheadedness just long enough to escape into the gardens of Versailles.

He found little peace among the exquisite never-ending fields of green and towering hedges, spattered with gravel pathways and ornate gazebos. A large gathering of nosy aristocrats followed him everywhere he went. Just as in New York, women giggled in curiosity while the men approached and made ignorant comments. José yearned for a loaded opium pipe, a soft bed, and one of Noemi's interviews.

As the sun began to set, José managed to find solitude in a smallish greenhouse. He knew Dewitt, in the form of Manuel, would be looking for him, so he curled up on a bench and tried to fall asleep. The sound of gravel underneath padded feet pushed the exhausted pilot out of his stupor and into an even worse mood. He was only aware of one door to the greenhouse so he decided to stay as still as possible in the hope that the intruder would fail to notice him.

"That was quite the show you put on back there," somebody said in Spanish with an eastern accent, "Almost makes all the years I've been waiting for you worth it."

José rolled over and took in a small, stringy Asian woman. Her nose was upturned, her cheeks sharp enough to cut glass. She donned a servant's smock, green skirt and brown corset.

"Waiting for me?"

"You're José, the one who landed today in the plane?"

"Look, I'm just trying to relax."

"You're after Diane, right?"

José bolted to his feet, "What did you just say?"

The woman smiled smugly, crossed her arms, and repeated, "You're after Diane, right?"

"Who are you? Did she send you?"

"Name's Li Mei, and no, she didn't send me, though I'm well aware who she is. Thought you and her were the only people who could harness chronological transference, did you?"

-

CHAPTER

19

April, 1685

Zula cowered next to Diane, pleading, "Make it stop, make it stop, make it stop..." The building continued to rumble, the remaining light fixtures crashed to the floor. Zula grabbed Diane's hand in desperation. The Cahokian leader tore her hand away and demanded at the top of her lungs, "Open the door! Do it, now!"

Zula clicked a hidden button somewhere on the sleeve of the ghoulish costume, activating the drawbridge motor which began its descent. At first, the two could only see a haze that vibrated to the ear-splitting explosions. The Cochimi camp was in the process of being carpet bombed. Zula took off the black cloth mask by pulling at the string-lights. Diane could finally see the face of a middle-aged man, gaunt and rashy. His bottom lip quivered as he watched his domain razed.

"ETA?" Diane said in English, keeping her domineering gaze on Zula. Upon hearing Diane speak, the spiritual fraud prostrated himself in front of her, blubbering for mercy. Hatha's soothing voice buzzed into Diane's ear, "We should be there."

"Land right outside the drawbridge and come inside. No hostiles that I'm aware of," Diane switched to Sauk so the trembling Zula could understand, "Watch."

Zula scrambled up and watched in terror as a massive armed helicopter hovered down in front of the drawbridge. Zula promptly shat his suit and fell to his knees. Behind this mechanical dragon, countless others just like it was patrolling the skies above the smoking Cochimi camp. Fires blazed, smoke rose, and the screams of half burnt people were barely audible over the sounds of beating helicopter blades. Diane's head slumped to the floor gratefully as three Cahokian medics rushed in, accompanied seconds later by two heavily armed Cahokian soldiers, both pointing machine guns at the shit stained man in the funny looking costume.

Before 1681, Zula had been a recluse, living on the fringe of the Cochimi territory, surviving by trading tools and totems that he made. When the influx of technology had entered the Baja peninsula, he had taken to it instantly. He hoarded as much as he could, spending most of 1683 and 1684 traveling around the expanding Cahokian Empire. The Cochimi were already an intensely independent, but gullible people so it was easy for him to build a temple outfitted with a complex array of electrical wiring. Cannibalism had always been a sick fantasy of his, discovered as a boy when his abusive father had forced him to eat the flesh of a dead Spaniard.

The medics loaded Diane onto a stretcher. On her direction, they brought her directly to the side of Zula and paused, allowing her to lean over and say one last thing, "Onawa Greenrock."

The two soldiers grabbed Zula and tossed him over the edge of the drawbridge onto the starved porpoises. His wails were cut short as the cetacean mob dragged him underwater and devoured him piece by piece.

Inside the helicopter, the medical team tended to Diane's wounds, as she dictated orders to one of the soldiers, "Destroy that temple."

The soldier jumped into the cockpit and instructed the pilot. A missile launcher hanging on the bottom of the vehicle rotated towards the temple and in a split second the shimmering edifice no longer existed. Hatha buzzed in Diane's ear, "You're on your way back."

"No, I'm going south."

"Ma'am..."

"I'll be fine, there are things that need to be done down there."

The line was silent. Then she heard Chaska's voice over the earpiece, "We're handling things just fine. You need to recuperate, I'll keep you informed."

The soldier returned from the cockpit, "There's a group of about twenty Cochimi fleeing north on horseback. What's your order?"

Diane knew Chaska and Hatha had heard the report and were also awaiting her decision. She could let them go, but that would risk news of this operation getting out to the rest of Cahokia before it could be tempered. "Eliminate them."

The soldier ran back into the cockpit and their helicopter propelled northward. The thundering silence from her earpiece made her squirm.

Throughout the flight back to Cahokia city, Diane's body absorbed adrenaline and pain medication. The monsters' squadron leaders kept in contact with her throughout the rest of the mission which didn't last more than two hours. The Cochimi people were now wiped off the face of the planet.

Upon arrival to Cahokia City, the medics hurried her to the best hospital out of the three. For the next week, doctors worked on Diane, doing her up with casts, IV drips, and anesthesia. Since no Cahokians had more than four years of expertise with the medical technology she had brought, Diane's arm cast had to be redone twice. Nikan didn't leave her side the entire time, ensuring that messengers sent on Diane's behalf were relaying the correct instructions.

After a month, Diane was ready to walk, so it was time to attend a High Council meeting. She ordered Nikan to bring her to the chambers in a wheelchair, even though she was fully capable of going there on her own. She knew that she would need all the sympathy she could get.

The only members of the High Council that lasted from the original twelve-person Council were Chaiton and Wabaunsee. The other nine, excluding the late Onawa, still served on the general council but had fallen to the wayside as seventeen new Chiefs were elected. The resident old-timers Chaiton and Wabuansee held the most clout, but a relatively young Navajo leader named Askook continuously challenged them.

Nikan wheeled Diane in the chambers. The entire High Council was present. Diane cleared her throat.

"Before men and women walked the Earth, there was Coyote. Not just Coyote, there were other animals, but Coyote was the cleverest one of them all. Yes, Bison, Wolf, Buffalo, Moose, Bear, Cougar, even Eagle, could outpace Coyote, but that didn't stop him from trying to trick them. One day, Mother Earth found Coyote lapping water from a stream and gifted him a stick to carry in his mouth. On the end of this stick, there was a flame that never extinguished and allowed Coyote to cook his food, scare off predators, and find his way in the dark. Soon he dominated the plains, and all other beings feared and respected him. Then one day, Fox, Coyote's closest friend, asked for the stick. Coyote, thinking that his friend Fox was trustworthy because he had a bushy tail and whiskers just like him, lent the stick to Fox with the condition that he return it as soon as whatever he wanted to do was over. Fox agreed and ran off with the fire-stick. He began to burn down the forests and kill innocent defenseless creatures. However, as promised, Fox returned the fire-stick to Coyote. Seeing their ravaged home, the rest of the animals, Wolf, Buffalo, Moose, Bear, Cougar, even Eagle declared war upon Coyote, even though Fox was the arsonist."

Askook, the square-faced, arrogant Navajo leader chuckled, "I'm unfamiliar with this proverb. Is Cahokia the Coyote and the Cochimi the Fox? Which means that you're Mother Earth?"

"Okay, change it so Coyote found the stick! I went behind your back, yes. I employed the Monsters when we had agreed never to make executive decisions without the entire High Council behind it. I didn't have a choice! It was either this or perish at the hands of a cannibalistic cult."

Askook bobbed his head, "We all heard the recording of your orders."

"How?"

Askook bobbled his head condescendingly, "Proprietary. We're impressed by the Monsters, yet, the chain of command was broken. You had a choice. You could have stayed with Cochimi as their prisoner until negotiations had soured and then, most likely, we would have authorized the use of such force."

"I didn't want to take that chance of them eating me."

"The rest of us would have taken that chance. You're the only one with a radio receiver embedded in your skull," Askook started strolling around the room, gesticulating wildly, "Zula was a crazed leader who happened to catch on at the right time. Frankly, the British worry me more than the Cochimi ever did. Why are we still trading with them? They are just as culpable for atrocities against our people as the French and the Spanish."

Diane could see many elders nodding in agreement. It was not time to mince words.

"The French and Spanish forced our hand. They refused to establish trade with us, but the British did not. We need a European ally, and England is about to go through a difficult time politically, so if we can help them, we'll be able to open up trade to the rest of the continent."

Askook was ready for this, "You are so familiar with their ways. How are we supposed to trust you when you tell us about their *continent*? We've heard your stories about other lands. I will admit, the black slaves they bring support your theory but a faraway land to the west, filled with hundreds of millions of people! Preposterous! I can no longer sit back and listen idly as you fill Cahokians' heads with propaganda."

"Asia is a real place..."

"Then why haven't you shown us? Why have we only dealt with those to the east?"

Diane bit her lip. It would have been easy to expose Cahokia to Asia, however she didn't think either party was ready. Before she could think of a response, Askook continued, "Time and time again, you've moved ahead without the consent of the High Council, against the government that you helped create! We're thankful for what you've brought us. We were dying by the thousands from disease and war when you came and you've dragged us out of that pit. Even though you won't tell us why you've done all of this, you chose us, so we must conclude that the Great Spirit brought you to us because we are the chosen people. Not the French, not the Spanish, not those who live across the sea, and especially not the British. If we can afford to attack in cold blood one of our own tribes then it's more than reasonable that we can once and for all push the British off of our land."

The rest of the elders were moved. Diane looked to Chaiton with fleeting hope, but he avoided eye contact. She sighed, "If this is your decision, then let it be so. We'll push the British off, but I urge you to negotiate as much as possible before we commit any violence."

"Like you did with the Cochimi?" accused Askook. Diane snapped her finger and pointed at Askook, "Exactly. Except the British don't eat people."

José and Li Mei stood in the middle of the greenhouse.

"What year are you from?"

"I was born in the year sixteen-"

Li Mei fell silent as two royal sentries entered the greenhouse, strode up to José, and asked him firmly to accompany them back to the palace. José looked helplessly at Li Mei, who bowed her head demurely.

In the palace, Dewitt scolded José repeatedly for ditching the afternoon's events. José apologized halfheartedly, too dazed to defend himself. After, he grabbed the lapel of the nearest servant and demanded opium to be delivered to his room with great haste. José mollified himself into oblivion, shrouded in a thick cloud of poppy paradise.

The next day, sprawled on top of the gaudy covers of an even gaudier canopy bed, José fluttered awake only to find a dull, raggedy servant standing in the middle of his room, holding a large metal pot with both hands. A horrific pissy stench emanated from the man and José grabbed a pillow to block his nose. "What do you want?"

"Monsieur," replied the hireling, "Master Manuel informed me that you like to relieve yourself in the mornings."

The large pot was a piss bucket whose contents were dangerously close to sloshing onto the floor as the servant moved towards the edge of the bed. "No! No!" cried José, putting a hand up, "I'll just use the gardens."

The piss catcher bobbed his head respectfully, spilling a bit of fermenting urine on the carpet and trundled towards the door. José cursed his new lodgings, flummoxed that a place could be simultaneously so beautiful and rancid.

"Hey, do you know a Li Mei?" José asked the piss catcher who wobbled to a stop, spilling more urine. He shook his head, "Describe her."

"Asian, small, skinny?"

"There are no Orientals here, sire." The man hefted the container out of the room. The stench remained, now infused into the carpets. Soon Manuel fetched José, bringing him down to the palace grounds where the plane was sitting on a patch of grass. A crowd of two hundred people gathered around the edges. None were recognizable.

"Mechanics check," grumbled Manuel, "they want to watch."

"They wanna watch me check the engine?"

"No, they're here to play croquet, while you check the engine."

After a draining few hours of fielding repetitive, childish queries while trying to perform what would have been a routine thirty-minute engine check, Dewitt and King Louis arrived, followed by an army of nobles. José looked for Li Mei but could only see a sea of white. Dewitt signaled to José that it was time to prepare for take-off, this time with King Louis aboard.

José readied the plane while the Sun King gave a curt speech, filled with adorations to god and country. It seemed as if nothing could be done in the aristocracy without a dramatic address. Everybody needed their moment to be seen and heard. Dewitt and Manuel entered with the monarch in tow. Louis's belly barely fit into the other cockpit seat, however soon they were racing down the green and sputtered skywards. The motor sounded worse than ever. The first half of the flight was rather dull, at least to every passenger but Louis. Then the esteemed majesty claimed that he could see Russia.

"Still France," corrected José.

The King frowned. José tacked on politely, "your eminence."

"Are you quite sure? I see Slavic hovels in the distance."

José glanced back to Dewitt for guidance. The statesman ducked his head to give José permission to proceed with caution. "At most, your eminence, one can see, from this altitude, 50 leagues give or take in any direction." José tilted the plane upwards, enlarging the view.

"Yes, but we've traveled far, no? Which means that that could be Russia. I know what French villages look like and that is not one. Look at that church!"

"We've been heading south, your majesty..."

Dewitt chimed in, "Maybe your directional device is malfunctioning, that could be Russia, perhaps Poland?"

"Sure. Could be Russia."

The Mediterranean Sea loomed in front of them. José bit his tongue. After they landed, the mass of Louis' subjects congratulated him as he dished about how destitute Russia appeared. The King made sure to publicly shake José and Dewitt's hands, which gave José an opportunity to ask the King a question, "Do you know Li Mei? Oriental woman? Yay high?"

"Li Mei is one of my many advisors. A great lay, when she's in the mood..." The King's nonchalant attitude regarding mistresses soon made sense to José who had Manuel explain. Louis' first marriage was with Maria Theresa of Spain, who happened to be his double first cousin, meaning that they shared the same set of grandparents. It wasn't kismet, rather a political move to end a lengthy war between Spain and France and further meld the House of Habsburg and Bourbon. Beyond bringing peace between these two superpowers, Maria's main objective was to produce healthy male heirs, which proved difficult. Poor Maria had given birth to six children during her reign but only one had survived to adulthood, also named Louis. Louis Jr was currently a shit-eating spoiled twenty-four-year-old who obsessed over art more than politics.

Even during Maria's life, Louis Sr had a dugout of primped noble women through which he rotated shamelessly. The King had held a secret marriage soon after his first wife's demise with Francoise d'Aubigne, whose fervent devotion to Catholithism and homosexual tendencies drove the court mad. More importantly, it gave Louis the moral high ground to fool around.

"Where could I find her?" asked José submissively.

"Try the baths."

The baths were a large array of connecting swimming pools and showers, the only room beyond the King and Queen's that had indoor plumbing. It was really the only place to wash oneself, however it was seldom used for anything but sweaty trysts and horny spectators. José discovered this when he walked in on a man touching himself carnally to a set of what looked like sisters pleasuring each other. José didn't have the heart or the stomach to confirm the proximity of their relation. Still, no sign of Li Mei.

After searching and questioning almost all of Versailles, José did his nightly ritual of puffing on opium and zonking out. The next morning, he arose to find Dewitt sitting on the side of his bed.

"Today, we fly to see Charles. It is paramount that we convince him to finance and sanction our mission against Cahokia. Louis is already with us, and I don't see Charles being difficult to convince, but we mustn't lose focus.

Charles must see the value in this expedition, because without Spain, we have nothing."

"I understand," José yawned, "but I'm not sure how much longer we can use the plane. The whale oil is eating through the engine. It sounded horrible when we flew Louis."

"I'm sure it'll last one more flight."

"We'll see."

"When will you tell me the truth?"

"The truth about what?"

"Where you're from. What happened between Diane and you?"

José murmured, "I can't…"

"You can't what?"

José took a deep breath. Diane had duly warned him of the consequences of telling somebody of their temporal travels, but it was exhausting keeping it a secret. Maybe, telling Dewitt would make things easier.

"It's a long story. I don't think that you'll…"

One of Charles' smartly dressed maids stepped suddenly into the room. José immediately stopped talking. "The King is ready," said the maid.

The crowd for Charles' flight was even larger than Louis's. Ahead, the Spanish King waited dumbly in his wheelchair. The crowd watched in glee as ceremonial pleasantries passed between Dewitt and Charles, with the Dutchman making most of the conversation and the Spaniard grunting occasionally. José edged over to the maid that had brought them, "the chair won't fit…"

"We will assist his ascent."

With the help of the entire maid staff and the moral support of the hundreds of onlookers, Charles made it onto the plane, crawling on his hands and knees. The runway was cleared and José, Dewitt, and King Charles the Second of Spain lifted off into the hazy French atmosphere.

Charles was propped up in the neighboring cockpit seat, staring out the window while drool ran down from his mouth. Dewitt hovered nervously at the door, trying to gauge the King's indecipherable reactions. The engine rumbled.

"Your Majesty, what think you? God's domain, in all its glory?"

The King's drool disconnected from his gaping mouth and wetted his silk shirt.

"Your Majesty?"

José took a closer look at the King's face. It seemed a different shade of pale and the eyes seemed more glazed. "Uhh, you better check his pulse..."

The Dutch Statesman felt the King's neck and his eyes grew wide.

"Land, goddammit, land!"

By the time the plane's wheels touched down, it was too late. Air travel had proved too stressful for the frail homunculus. José and Dewitt sat in silence. The late King Charles' dead weight strained the multitude of extra seat belts. They could hear horses and cheering crowds galloping towards the grounded plane. José tried the ignition, but it sputtered and failed, clunking horribly. The whale oil had finally eaten its way through the fuel tank. Dewitt ran a hand through his thinning hair, "You're from the future, aren't you?"

-

April, 1685

"What's your relationship like with the Swallow?" Diane asked Nikan. The two were sitting on the top of Diane's four-story house, looking out over Cahokia. The city had expanded quickly, stretching all the way to either side of Lake Michigan, or Lake Patowa as the Cahokians called it.

"Dyani likes me," said Nikan, who sat with a pen and pad. Dyani was the head editor for the Swallow, Cahokia's national news organization.

"What's the worst thing someone could do? What'd make people hate him the most?"

"Him?"

"Whoever."

"Well, for a man, probably having sex with a woman while she's on her period."

Diane felt rather let down, "How many wives does Askook have?"

"Diane...You're going to dig yourself a deeper grave."

"How many?"

"At the moment, four."

"Okay, here's what I want you to do," Diane moved to the edge of her seat, "Call the Sparrow with an anonymous tip-"

"They might recognize my voice?"

"You'll make the call from my radio, they won't know who's calling. You'll say that you witnessed Askook fucking one of his wives, pick whichever, maybe the oldest, but that you saw that after, his dick was red. Tell them that you saw bruises on her arm, so it seems forced."

Nikan looked up from the notepad, unsettled, "Did you see this?"

"Of course not," Diane said with a malevolent grin, "but you did."

"They won't ask for proof?"

"They're a new organization, they make more profit when they sell more papers," Diane leaned back in her chair, clasping her hands together, "Did you get those barter statistics with New England for last quarter?"

"Of course," Nikan extracted several sheets of paper from a folder on the table. Diane nodded, "Exports first, please."

"Two hundred veloks of potato, three hundred veloks of avocados, forty-five of vanilla, six thousand tobacco-"

Diane held up her hand to pause Nikan. She quickly did some mental conversions from veloks, the Cahokians' unit of volume, to tons. "Okay, we should increase potatoes and vanilla, but decrease tobacco. Skip to vehicles."

Nikan moved down the paper, "Ten electric bikes, fifty mechanical bikes, one bisoon."

"One bisoon? Who the fuck gave the British a bisoon?"

"A military squadron from the Inuit faction."

"Fuckin' Eskimos! What did they get in return?"

"Ten African slaves..."

"Did we not outlaw slavery?" Diane buried her head in her hands, "How about weapons?"

"No record, but I did hear talk of a deal between the Susquehannock and Jamestown. A small arsenal for a collection of rare fruit they call a banana?"

"We can't be giving weapons to our soon-to-be enemies! What type?"

Nikan pursed her lips, "Rifles."

"Thank god. Impose an embargo on British trade for vehicles and weapons. Notify the HC immediately, they'll have to agree."

Nikan scribbled on a notepad furiously, "It seems as if there's some problem arising in the South East. The Chocta's local economy has tanked, money is losing its value, but nobody understands why."

"Didn't two new mints just open up there? It's probably inflation."

"Inflation?"

"They're printing too many Fuzi. Shut them down. Tax them a little harder next quarter."

Nikan jotted all of this down. The front door radio buzzed onto the roof's intercom.

"Can I come in?"

Diane's heart jumped.

"Out, out," she shooed Nikan out the door, then pressed a button to open the door for Chaska. He made his way to the roof, pausing at the sight of her. Each waited for the other to start. She coughed.

"Askook is misguided," said Chaska finally.

Diane could exhale once more, "What are you going to do?"

"Attack the British. I have to follow the High Council, even if I believe with every fiber of my being that we shouldn't."

"Do you think I was wrong to bomb the Cochimi?"

"I would have done the same. So would Askook. He's just being opportunistic."

Diane pointed to a humming solar powered refrigerator full of refreshments, but Chaska shook his head. She was relieved that she could finally speak to Chaska alone.

"I'm glad you agree with me. I fear my absence has allowed a fox into the hen house."

"Chickens live outside..."

"Never mind. You've come here for a reason?"

Chaska nodded, "If I'm to understand our position on a global scale, at least from our military's success against Spain and France, Cahokia is poised and ready to move overseas. Askook and other members of the High Council have already approached me with questions of ships and large planes. They fully intend to drive out the Europeans, but they also want to advance into their lands. Several gliders are on their way across the western and eastern oceans. Not with weapons, thank the Great Spirit, but if they confirm that those civilizations are less advanced..."

"They're definitely less advanced."

The warrior general took a deep breath, "What happens in your time?"

"You know I can't tell you that."

"You must! I need to make a decision, and you have the gift of foresight."

Diane moved to the edge of the seat, flustered, "But I don't! The world I left is long gone."

"I'm not asking you to go back there! I'm asking you to tell me what might happen in our world so I can know how to move forward. What did the Europeans do with us? What happened to my people?"

Chaska seemed so insistent, so desperate, Diane considered giving in. He was just trying to ensure a safe future for his people. But where to begin?

"Give me your radio," Diane demanded, so Chaska immediately handed over the small metal transmission box. She chucked it off the roof.

"Are you willing to risk your sanity?"

"I am."

"When I come from, the world was...will be...is a very different place. There are vestiges of the powers that exist today, but obviously new ones arose. Europeans dominated the world, establishing colonies throughout the world. The French and Dutch are currently supreme, but in roughly a century the British will rise to the top. Their exploitation of less advanced nations would continue until the early 1900s. The remnants of the European colonies would grow into new, independent countries which would rebel from their colonial masters.

By the time these new states came to be, the Native population of this land would have been killed off, enslaved, or completely assimilated. A vast majority of the blacks would be slaves bought in Africa and sailed over. This process has already begun. The new countries wouldn't continue the slave trade for long, but they would keep using slaves on their plantations for centuries after. Institutionalized racism spurred on by profit. The land that is now Cahokia would become three distinct countries, Mexico, formerly Spanish, Canada, formerly British and French, and The United States of America, formerly British. In the early 1900s, there would be two great wars involving many of the European, American, African, and Asian countries that would result in a power struggle between The United States of America and Russia, a nation in Northern Eurasia. The United States would ultimately win and dominate the economic, political, and social world stages for many decades.

"However, soon natural resources would run dry. The United States and other super powers like China would lose power due to massive energy, food, and water shortages. Around the turn of the twenty-second century, two nations would emerge supreme. Canada and Brazil. Brazil would have been an ex-Portuguese nation in South Cahokia. Both have the largest natural holds of freshwater and leveraged this financially to get ahead in desalination. Eventually, all of the major corporations would move to Canada or Brazil, due to their access to freshwater. Of course, like throughout history, the two wouldn't share the spotlight. When I left, Canada and Brazil were at each other's necks."

Chaska didn't wait to ask, "What is left of our culture in this future?"

"Barely anything. Some places use your names and design their buildings lazily with totems. As for your people, there are only a few million left."

"A few million?! That's not so bad."

"Most of them will be extremely poor and completely assimilated. That's not going to happen now. The reason I came back, Chaska, is to save the world from the pain and terror that Europeans will inflict upon the rest of the world. Their desire for wealth would drive them to use their superior technology to exploit the rest. I want to give the indigenous people of America the ability to fight back and establish a peaceful status quo, as well as introduce sustainable technology earlier on."

Chaska didn't speak for several minutes, while his knee bounced. Finally, he asked, "Do many people from your era travel through time?"

"Only a few."

"What's stopping them from coming back and preventing all of your progress?"

"It's not as simple as that. The minute I traveled back in time, I created an alternate timeline," Diane grinned, thrilled to nerd out, "The world I left exists still, just in a different dimension. I created the split when I arrived. We live in a new dimension."

"Can you get to the old dimension?"

"Not with the physics I'm aware of. Too many paradoxes."

"Paradoxes?"

"With only one timeline, time travel becomes too messy. Let's say you go back in time and kill your father before you were born. How would your mother have you if not for your father? If you don't exist because you were never born, how would you be able to time travel in the first place to kill your father?"

Chaska scratched his head, "That doesn't make sense."

"Exactly."

"Could somebody from the future of this dimension travel back and try to stop you?"

"Potentially."

Chaska was obviously confused but tried his best not to show it.

"Back to the plan," Diane filled up her cup with juniper tea, "We need to set history on a course where Cahokia makes contact with everybody else as peacefully as possible so the spread of technology is balanced equally throughout. My native time was peaceful for the most part. Little squabbles here and there were blown up by the media, but in reality, fighting between countries, mostly

Canada and Brazil, was done non-physically. We had reached a point where all the major world powers had comparable technology. There was disparity, sure some poor countries had little clean water, but the internet allowed for governments and private companies to watch over everything. It was far from perfect, but it was the best we could do. Now, we have an opportunity to improve on that. The only reason that Europe was able to conquer the world is because they had a scientific revolution and worshipped capitalism. Imagine if Cahokia did the same thing but instead of treating their hosts with hostility and brutality, they educate the world and the people build upon it. We'd rid ourselves of wealth inequality, solve global warming, eliminate political unrest, extend our lifespans, remove the burden of overpopulation!"

Diane realized that she was standing, half shouting, half preaching to Chaska, who looked bewildered.

"What's the internet?" he asked.

"Something I have yet to introduce. Not until everybody is at the same level."

"Okay, but what is it?"

"You're not ready for it!"

"You can still tell me the idea!"

"I can't!"

Chaska leaned back, "My military is at your disposal, if you tell me what the internet is."

Diane fell back into her seat. She wanted to punch him. Or fuck him, she couldn't decide.

"The internet is a complex system of computer networks that shares data by connecting each device with a set of communication protocols."

Chaska rolled his eyes, "In Sauk, please."

"It's the ability to share information across the world in a split second. It's the world's biggest library in one book. It's an instantaneous postal service but instead of carrier pigeons or smoke signals, it uses radio waves."

The warrior general showed no emotion. Diane barreled ahead, "It's a blessing and a curse. In my era, it was a tool of science and learning for the first few decades of its existence. Then it started going south."

"South of where? New Spain?"

"Sorry, it went badly. People became addicted to it. There's no surprise why. Anything and everything could be accessed instantly with little effort."

"I don't understand why that's a bad thing."

Diane countered, "It's really easy to learn to live with new technology, but almost impossible to learn to live without it. People were always distracting themselves, placating their inner thoughts. Consequently, businesses formed around capitalizing on this constant distraction. Companies allowed people to use their information or trade information with each other, but these companies would monitor their customers' actions. Then they would sell these observations about people to other companies so they could learn more and more about them, allowing rampant manipulation of consumerism, politics, and social interaction."

Chaska's head was spinning, "So why would you introduce this at all?"

"Because, soon, we won't be able to move forward without it. All we can hope to do is control it as much as possible."

Chaska looked like he needed some water, so she poured him a glass. They both reclined and thought deeply, Chaska on how fearful he was on what was to come and Diane on how to properly stage a coup d'état.

José groaned, delirious. His back was twitching with cramps and bruises. He hadn't had the opportunity to sleep on anything but slimy stone for days or weeks. He wasn't really sure how long he'd been in this tiny jail cell. The last thing he remembered from the outside world was the chaotic aftermath of Charles' death. The mob of people had arrived on the plane, expecting to see the Spanish monarch safe and sound. When they found him dead, they grabbed Dewitt and José, pulled them violently out of the plane, and beat the living shit out of them. José had woken up an indeterminable time later inside a stone prison too small to lay down fully. Countless belligerent rats kept him company.

At one point, José thought he had gone blind from his beat down, but a guard holding a torch had marched to the cell bars just a few hours ago, shoved a moldy piece of bread through the bars, and departed. Then existential dread paired with opium withdrawals brought on a bout of panic attacks. He couldn't keep the moldy bread down which ended up on the floor and attracted more rats. José began to see things.

First, Sarah visited him. His ex was dressed in her old goth uniform, black overalls with chains and an excessive amount of eyeliner. She stood over him, arms crossed, a disapproving smirk smeared across her pretty little face, "This is what you deserve, you know that?"

"Why?" grumbled back José, on his back with his legs propped up the wall.

"Are you serious? All those times you would call me just to come over for a blowjob and a cuddle? What about a date, a nice dinner?"

"I thought you enjoyed hanging out with me..."

"I did, I did," Sarah admitted, then squatted down to him, "But then you got boring. Everything was the same. Always about you. Fly your dad's planes, flirt with Candace, smoke weed. That's not a life, José."

"Sounds like a pretty good life to me."

"If you hadn't slept on the plane, you wouldn't have gone with Diane."

"If you had gone to the Bronco instead, I wouldn't have drunk so much!"

Sarah snorted, "You broke my heart long before I started hanging with Kyle."

At the mention of his arch nemesis' name José coughed involuntarily and violently. After a minute, he opened his eyes to find that Sarah had been replaced by Kyle Peterson. José glared at the annoyingly tall and handsome boy, wavy bleach blonde hair falling over a tan chiseled face. All the girls in Capron had fought over him at one point, so all boys had hated him with a passion. José had walked onto the back porch of one of their homecoming parties and witnessed Kyle and Sarah entangled together with little clothing. At least Kyle had the decency to have clothes on during this vision.

"Sup, brother," Kyle said cheerfully, always in an upbeat mood.

"I'm not your fucking brother, asshole."

"Didn't mean to harsh your vibe, man. Like I said, she said you guys were done."

"Why the fuck do you talk like that? Weren't you born in Iowa? Wake up! You're not from California!" shouted José.

Kyler Peterson shrugged, unfazed, "Dude, Cali's the spot. Used to visit my cuz out in Malibu."

His surfer dreamboat intonation was the focus of many of José's friends' impersonations. José began to tear up, remembering all the good times with Bernie, Phil, and Gary.

"Why you cuttin' onions, dawg? You wanna talk about it?"

"Shut the hell up, piece of shit!" yelled José, "You slept with my girlfriend!"

"People aren't property, bro."

"Tell that Piero..."

Kyle Peterson flipped his notorious hair, "My boy, Piero! Where's that little dude?"

José gagged. Even in his imagination, Kyle was better friends with people that preceded him by more than three centuries. José blinked and sighed in relief. Kyle Peterson had been replaced by Noemi, who wore exactly what she did that glorious day in the bordello. "Can you stay here for a while? You're the first one I've actually wanted to see."

"Why can't you just walk out of here?" Noemi said with a sweet smile.

"What?"

"You need to get up and walk away."

"I'm not sure what you mean. I'm in a prison cell?"

"All of this? It's too much." Noemi crossed her arms, leaned down, and placed her face close to José, "I love you, José, don't forget that." Then, she vanished. José cried and cried, his sobs echoing off into nothingness, until he heard footsteps and saw torchlight.

Two guards dragged José through a winding dungeon of unimaginable filth and despair. His legs had lost feeling long before their arrival so his feet limply thudded across the rough tile. He managed to peek at a few of his incarcerated neighbors through the torchlight, a series of wretched souls, hellishly disfigured and hunched.

The prison must have been immense because it took almost twenty minutes to exit into the light where José was blinded by the penetrating sunlight. He clenched his lids shut as hard as possible but his retinas still burned. He kept them closed for the next thirty minutes, resigning himself to his four other senses. José was pretty sure that he was outside, maybe in the palace gardens, hearing the birds chirp, smelling flowers and horse shit, and feeling the cool refreshing breeze. A few minutes later, he was inside with hundreds of voices all clamoring over each other in French and Spanish. The searing pain had passed so José ventured to open his eyes.

He found himself in a large circular room filled to the brim with audaciously decorated men jostling each other for a better view. Every single one was shouting over the next, trying to be heard over the rising din. If José could have lifted his arms high enough to cover his ears, he would have but the guards had fastened him with shackles to the arms of a chair in the middle of a room.

The famished pilot winced as the shouting increased to an unbearable level. The men were pointing at a bedraggled figure that was similarly hoisted onto a seat next to José. It took a full minute for José to realize that this shivering mess was Dewitt.

"Are you okay?" mouthed José. He had never seen the regal Dutchman look and smell so pathetic. Dewitt slowly elevated his head to José who gasped when he realized that Dewitt's left eye had been gouged out. All that was left was a bloody, scarred orifice. Dewitt gave a frail smirk.

The court fell completely silent. King Louis strolled in with a small horde of advisors and officials. The entire room remained respectfully quiet until the King had taken his spot on an obnoxious throne. There was a jostling for positions around the King by different royal advisors, bishops, and noblemen. Louis raised his hand and a court bailiff moved to the King's side and read off a decree, "Under the authority of the Louis Dieudonné de Bourbon, King of France, and the Roman Catholic Church, Dewitt van Oldenbarnevelt, for your involvement in the assassination of Charles the Second, King of Spain, you are sentenced to fifty years of indentured servitude to the Kingdom of France."

Dewitt stared straight ahead, unflinching. José suspected the adroit businessman had known that this would be his verdict. The bailiff cleared his throat and continued, "As for José of Cahokia, commander of the Flying Machine, for your involvement in the assassination of Charles the Second, King of Spain, you are sentenced to death by breaking wheel!"

An excited energy filled the room as if the bailiff had just announced a new kind of dessert had been added to the kitchen's menu. José bit his lower lip in an attempt to wake himself up. Maybe he was still in the dungeon and this was just another nightmare. Did they not have trials? When could he try to defend himself? Do they really think he was Cahokian? What in god's name was a breaking wheel? Dewitt seemed strangely unaffected and José came to the conclusion that the Dutchman had also known what José's fate would be.

"Silence! Silence!" yelped the bailiff, "The execution shall take place tomorrow, the twenty sixth of May, the year of our lord, sixteen eighty-five!"

The crowd cheered warmly, clapped politely, and wished King Louis a long life. The regal fat man rose, "The Lord hath seen fit to pardon Monsieur van Oldenbarnevelt for to his contributions to the crown. After careful examination and consultation, I have concluded that he held no malice for Charles, but that this dastardly savage he uses for a pilot is not only a deadly assassin but a Cahokian spy!"

The court jeered and several spit at José, who tried to get Dewitt's attention with some *pssts*. The Dutchman ignored José and kept rapt attention on the King.

"The Spanish are retreating from the Americas. Cahokia has shown their true nature. I shall no longer dally and keep you in suspense: The succession of the Spanish throne."

The courtiers leaned in.

"My late wife, may God rest her soul, was Charles' sister. If she was still with us, she would be devastated by the loss of her dear brother and my beloved brother in law. Our son, Louis, is my pride and joy. Louis? Come forth!"

Louis Jr, the shit-eating, spoiled prince pushed his way through the crowd and took his place next to his father. His face was vacant, his demeanor uncaring. His double chin wiggled as he waved to his subjects. King Louis slid his arm around Louis Jr's sloped shoulders.

"Despite our prayers, Charles never produced an heir and failed to stipulate any indication of the direction of the Spanish throne post mortem. As we all well know, the crown of Spain is passed according to cognatic primogeniture, which means that Louis here is the closest male descendent through his mother, the sister of the late Spanish King."

José could see many of the court subjects whispering to each other in befuddled tones. Louis saw this as well, "Come now! Let me calm your queries, I'm well aware of the negotiations of my marriage with Maria, those that dictated she would renounce her rights to Spanish succession. However, this clause was made conditional on the payment of five hundred thousand écus, a fee that was never received by me or any other member of the Kingdom of France. Therefore, I present and proclaim, on this extraordinary day, the new King of Spain, Louis de Bourbon! Huzzah!"

What in the actual fuck was going on? José's felt faint. He had been sentenced to death and now there was a goddamn coronation happening over his imminent grave.

After a long procession of hand kissing and oath swearing to the new King of Spain, José was carted off back to the dungeon. This time he left his eyes open on the trip, allowing him to clearly see the location of his incarceration. The underground entrance was in the very back corner of the palace grounds, so José made sure to whiff as much fresh air as possible before plunging back into the hellscape.

That night, José and the rats didn't sleep a wink. All he could think about was how much he wanted some opium. This made him even more depressed. He contemplated suicide but couldn't figure out how. There was nothing to hang himself with and the ceilings were too high. When the guard delivered his final meal, José asked, "What is the breaking wheel?"

"Ah, the breaking wheel," said the guard cheerfully, "its nomenclature denotes its exact purpose. You shall be strapped down to the spokes of a large wheel. The executioner shall take a mallet and hammer down your joints that hang betwixt the gaps one by one. This shall be repeated until the signal is given by the King and then the coup de grace! He shall hammer your abdomen and head until the sweet release of internal rest."

José considered asking the guard to kill him then and there, but the man scurried off to yell at a rather defiant Huguenot who wouldn't stop spouting prayers. José listened to the shouting cease abruptly, figuring the unfortunate Calvinist had been silenced by force. That was an idea! Maybe he could provoke the guard into killing him?

"Hey! Hey son of a dirty bitch! Son of a dirty Jew!"

Footsteps and torch light grew closer so José laid on more, "The protestant is right! You're nothing but a low down, cursed catholic pig!"

José readied himself for sweet release. He stopped midsentence when he saw that the person standing in front of his cell bars was not the guard, but Li Mei, holding a torch and the guard's keys.

She pushed the key into the lock and swung the door open, "He wouldn't have killed you. Just beaten you to a pulp. Can you walk?"

"Are you real?"

"Come on!" Li Mei pulled José up and helped him hurriedly limp down the dingy hallway. Once outside, Li Mei wasted no time in pushing José into an empty coffin on top of a carriage. "Pretend to be dead or you will be."

She covered her face in black cloth and spurred the horse drawn buggy towards the palace gates. Inside the coffin, José debated whether this was real or not. It certainly felt real. All this time looking for Li Mei and right before he had lost all hope she had swooped in and saved him. It seemed too good to be true.

José bumped around the wooden box for two hours before he felt the carriage come to a stop and heard the horse munching on an apple. Li Mei tore off the coffin lid and helped José out into a rustic moonlit barn, full of hay and clucking chickens.

"Where are we?" asked José. Li Mei laid him down in a soft pile of straw. "A few miles outside of Versailles. We won't stay long since they'll be looking for you, but we have an hour to rest."

"King Louis said you're his advisor and I asked pretty much everybody..."

"That was stupid. I try to keep a low profile. Nonetheless, here we are. You're quite the troublemaker, aren't you?"

"I didn't mean to kill Charles, I swear! He died in the plane!"

"I know, I know. I heard all about it the first time."

José squinted, "Cause you're also from the future, right?"

"Indeed, I am. But not your future. I was born in 1691, in Qing, under the Kangxi Emperor, Xuanye."

"Wait, you were born six years from now?"

Li Mei nodded, extracting a blanket from the back and covering José. "I will explain everything soon, my friend, but first you must rest. You've made quite your mark on history thus far, but you still have more to do."

-

CHAPTER

21

June, 1685

Askook stretched out on a fuzzy wolf hide, feeling every inch of his body relax. Steam billowed around him. Askook had commissioned a crew of some of the craftiest Lakota construction workers to build him a luxurious sweat lodge. Comfy animal hides and decadent stone dream catchers made the indigenous sauna look like the inside of a quartz geode.

The Navajo chief was a powerful man. His tribe was the largest to join Cahokia, plus the Apache, the cousins of the Navajo, had gifted their voting power to him which made Askook's sway on the High Council unprecedentedly strong.

Still, he missed the spacious valleys and snowy peaks of his homeland. Askook had made a promise to his tribe and the Apache to represent them to the best of his ability in Cahokia, which luckily was proving to be easy. Nobody wanted to fuck with the Navajo and the Apache, so nobody wanted to fuck with Askook.

He yawned, letting the fragranced hot steam into his lungs. Soon the British would be vanquished and Askook would reign supreme over half the world. Even Diane, the mystical all-knowing witch, had been neutralized.

Thirsty, Askook knocked on the side of the enclosure to signal one of his attendants to enter. Hopefully, Askook thought, it would be the cute little Enola with her tight butt and trembling lips. When nobody entered, Askook knocked again. Then again, harder this time. Somebody was going to get a whipping.

Askook stumbled out of the sweat lodge which was on top of his roof. The night sky was cloudless and the full moon showed that none of Askook's attendants were present. He grumbled, grabbed a flask of water from the storage bar right outside the sweat lodge entrance, and reentered, assuring himself that he would sell all of his slaves, except Enola, the next morning. Inside again, he sipped the water and settled back onto the wolf hide. Just as he began to drift off, he heard a noise outside.

"I had to get my own water! Get in here, now!"

No response, and nobody entered. He heard another noise, like something large being dragged. It was time to punish whatever impudent creature lay outside. He moved to the door but found that it wouldn't budge. He pushed harder. It was stuck. Askook banged on the wooden frame,

"If this is Moki, I'm going to starve you for a full moon cycle! Let me out! Unlock the door!"

Askook began to sweat for real. Desperate, he slammed his entire body against the door. It held fast. He tried over and over, only succeeding in injuring his shoulder. He rammed himself against other parts of the sweat lodge, but the Lakota architecture was sturdy, as per his request.

Sizzling water vapor permeated up through vents, reaching boiling temperatures. Askook sank to the floor, clawing helplessly at the side of his sweaty geode.

That next morning, the High Council gathered for their daily meeting. Chaiton and Wabaunsee discussed education reform and the incoming winter while the others filed in. Five minutes after the scheduled start of the meeting, the ten present members looked around. Askook and Tuskaloosa, chief of the mighty Choctaw, were absent.

"Well, they know the rules. Let's begin," said Chaiton, "Who has the itinerary?"

"Askook," replied Wabaunsee glumly.

"Maybe we can have an early day," Chaiton proposed, "Anybody have anything?"

Diane strutted into the chamber, followed closely by Nikan, Chaska, and twenty armed soldiers. The High Council members hopped to their feet. Even Chaushila, the ancient chief from the Western Yokuts pulled himself up from his wheelchair.

Diane stopped in the middle of the room and grimly addressed the High Council members, "One of Askook's servants found him inside his sweat lodge this morning suffocated and dehydrated. It appears as if he was locked inside all night. At first it was believed accidental, but upon further inspection, we suspect murder. Somebody must have locked the door from the outside and then turned up the steam. We're currently interrogating his entire staff, and we will hold off on announcing to the public until we've determined the culprit."

The High Council members were stunned. Chaiton spoke up first, "And Tuskaloosa?"

Diane tilted her head suspiciously at the Iowa chief, "Chief Tuskaloosa is missing. After discovering Askook, we're confirming the location of all High Council and General Council members. Does anyone have any information that will help us find Tuskaloosa?"

Several chimed in with places that they'd last seen him, which Nikan jotted down. Diane thanked them, then pointed to Chaska and his soldiers, "Because there's evidence of foul play in Askook's death and the fact that Tuskaloosa's missing, we have to activate a state of emergency. I really hate to do this, but until we find the assassin and the Choctaw Chief, each one of you will be accompanied by a member of Chaska's security force."

The High Council furiously protested, all except Chaiton who did nothing but stare at Diane. He knew what was happening.

"I'm sorry, I truly am!" Diane yelled above the others, "Askook was an influential man, Cahokia will not be the same without him. He had many enemies, so everybody's a suspect. I'm not going to rest until his death is righted."

The chiefs noticed how threateningly close Chaska's soldiers were. One by one, they began to understand. Chaiton sighed forlornly, "And what of the British?"

"Our siege of New England must be postponed until the end of the state of emergency. Your security details will escort you to your respective homes, where you will remain until further notice."

Chaushila raised a bony finger, "I have my own guards to defend me."

"Rules are rules," Diane retorted sharply, "You're in danger right now, and Chaska's men are here to maintain the integrity of Cahokia."

"What of our duties to Cahokia?" murmured the old man as he fell back into his wheelchair feebly. Two soldiers moved in and grabbed the back of his chair.

"As per the constitution, when all High Council members are incapacitated, the State Secretary assumes control until it's deemed appropriate for the High Council members to return. I believe Nikan is our current State Secretary."

Nobody dared to point out that they never remembered electing a State Secretary, but the message was clear.

Once José and Li Mei left France and entered Catalunya, Li Mei let them relax their ludicrous pace slightly but remained wary for they were in the kingdom of the late King Charles. Their carriage bumped along a dirt path, just a few miles from the shimmering Mediterranean. Both wore hooded cloaks in order to disguise themselves as monks.

"My family lives in Jinan, in Qing, which I believe you know as China. I will be born in six years. In twenty years, when I am fourteen, Cahokia will invade my homeland, killing and enslaving millions."

"How old are you now?" José asked, massaging his atrophied legs.

"Thirty. My parents were poor wheat farmers. Life was simple. My brothers and sisters and I would work in the fields and play in the evenings. When the Cahokians came, we could do nothing but watch our lives burn. We were Buddhists but if we didn't convert to the Cahokians' beliefs, they would destroy us, so we practiced our faith behind closed doors. The invaders brought machines that would till the fields for us, so we lost our livelihood. My family moved into the city to make more money, but technology had replaced everything. The Cahokians claimed they had brought us a blessing, but all we could see was widespread poverty and unemployment. There were too many of us to fit in the schools. I found a job working as a masseuse for rich Cahokians. I'm not sure how I got the job so easily, but I took it without a second thought. One of my clients was named Hatha who turned out to be quite close with Diane."

"So, you stole her time travel device and came back here?"

Li Mei scoffed, "I didn't know what it was. I thought I would be able to sell it. I didn't think a tyrant like her would miss such a small thing."

"Tyrant?"

She eyed José curiously, "How well do you actually know her?"

"Not well at all."

A passing troop of country folk bowed their heads at the faux-clergymen. José waited until they were out of earshot, "What will happen?"

"Cahokia will conquer the world under the guise of manifest destiny. Except theirs is not by Jesus, but Diane. I was her personal masseuse. She would get drunk and cry about being lonely. One night, she drank more than usual, it was some holiday or something. Her army general came to visit and she dismissed me. I forgot my oil so I returned to the room and overheard her talking to the man about you."

"Really? About me?"

"She was worried about you."

José grunted in surprise, but Li Mei qualified, "Not about your wellbeing, she was worried of your effects on history."

They rode in silence for an hour, as José fermented in uncertainty. More than anything, he wished to return to Tuscany, smoke a bagful of poppy, and snuggle with Noemi. Li Mei took out her time travel device and handed it to José. He handled it with great care, fearful that it would send them ricocheting to some unknown era.

"If you traveled back in time, you must know how the time travel device works?"

"Not really. I played with it for months, but it went off when I was on a motorbike."

"It needs acceleration to work, I think. We were on a plane. That same plane I was flying at Versailles."

Jose handed back the time travel device to Li Mei, who slipped it back into her pocket, "That makes sense. Still not exactly sure how to set the right destination."

"Explain to me why we have to go to West Africa again? Kingdom of what?"

"Kingdom of Koya. There's a colony of British allies that can get us to Cahokia."

"Cahokia!?"

Li Mei glanced at José in consternation, "To stop Diane, of course!"

Jose threw back his hood in consternation, "What are two people going to do against an entire empire? We need an army!"

"Diane is powerful because she has the gift of foresight. We also have that gift."

"We barely made it out of France alive!"

Li Mei reigned the horse to a stop, almost causing José to lose his balance. She reached around José's head and lifted his hood back over him, "She can get us back to our original timelines. We just have to get the answer out of her."

Would he really be able to hug Angel again?

"You're sure she can do that?"

"She knows a lot more about that device than you know."

The Kingdom of Koya, which José would have called Sierra Leone, was a long trek. They did it mostly on foot, with a short boat trip from Gibraltar. Morocco was torrid and chaotic. During their second week in Meknes, a group of Portuguese mercenaries sexually assaulted Li Mei while José was fetching food. They moved quickly on to the next town, and promptly exited the Kingdom of Fez into the rich Islamic Mali Empire.

In Europe, with their darker complexions José and Li Mei felt out of place, constantly drawing odd looks. In Mali, a wealthy epicenter of trade and Islam, the two blended into the diverse spectrum of merchants who frequented the cultural oasis.

They passed through Timbuktu where they saw giant mosques built from mud and heard tales of an ancient king whose wealth was so vast that, on his pilgrimage to Mecca, he had ruined the entire North African economy by being too generous.

For food, Li Mei would kill small animals with a sling. She was deadly accurate with the device, two thick pieces of twine attached in the middle by a small pouch that could hold a rock. José watched in fascination as she flung projectiles at whatever she wished and almost always found her target.

Li Mei and José grew close. They both had endured a similar ordeal and shared a common enemy. They liked to compete on who could learn the local language faster, soon becoming hyperpolyglots, which wasn't a rare thing in Africa at this time. Their progression south had been slower than Li Mei had wanted since the gold she had stolen from Versailles quickly ran dry and they were forced to work for food and lodging. Due to lack of funds, José quit opium cold turkey. For maybe the first time since his formative years, José's mind was unfogged. Still, the thought of the road ahead and unforgiving withdrawals gave him many sleepless nights.

In early November, 1685 they reached the Kingdom of Koya. It was a mountainous stretch of land that started inland with spattering of tiny little hovels inhabited by the poorest but nicest people José had ever encountered. As they trekked towards the ocean, larger, Mediterranean houses replaced the hovels.

Hundreds milled by, though none paid any heed to the newcomers. A large clay arch welcomed them with big painted letters: *Wanduni ro yɔpɔwa*

"Any idea what that means?" José gestured to the sign.

"Probably the name of the town."

Li Mei was incorrect. *Wanduni ro yɔpɔwa* was not the name of the town. It meant *Man Market* in the Temne language. They were about to enter the largest port for trans-Atlantic slave trade on the entire coast of Africa.

-

November, 1685

"I'm just fed up with it, really," Nikan vented to Diane as they leaned against a balcony of the capital building of Etowah, the most populous Cahokian city within a hundred-mile radius of Jamestown. Below them, hundreds of Cahokians and British mingled together. Chamber musicians and tribal flutists struggled to stay in time with each other. It was awkward but charming. This was the celebration of the official treaty between Jamestown (by extension England) and Cahokia. Diane was too elated to listen carefully, "Huh?"

"The Aztecs and Incas are stubborn. I don't want another Cochimi on our hands, but their infighting with the local authorities is starting to get out of hand."

"Relax, Nikan, they will come around. It's only been a year since the Spanish left."

"You've seen the numbers, it'll be hard to control them if they revolt."

Diane gave Nikan her full attention, "Masses cannot organize and are useful only to a point. The Aztecs or the Incas outnumbered the Spanish by a thousand to one, but they remained loyal for so long because the Spanish could organize in the right way. They placed obedient politicians in all the high places, never let any useful, rebellious information spread easily between their subjects, and built up their colonies' economies to a point where the people forgot how to live without it. We're doing the same thing but better. Relax! Enjoy the day, it's a big milestone."

Someone behind them cleared their throat. Diane and Nikan turned to find Francis Howard, fifth Baron of Effingham, the current Crown Governor of Virginia. He was average height with a crow-like face framed by the ever-smelly curly wig that all Europe officials insisted on wearing at all times. "A toast is in order, if you ladies would like a libation?"

It took a moment for Diane to mentally switch to English, a language that she didn't speak much anymore. Drinks were passed around and clinked.

"When can we expect the first voyage? King James is anxious."

"He's asking about scheduling," Diane related to Nikan, "I'll handle it."

Nikan smiled, bobbed her head to the Governor, and departed. Francis frowned, "Where is she going? Did I break etiquette?"

"No, no, Nikan is a busy woman. You can direct your questions to me."

"Splendid. So, timeline?"

"The first trip will be done by flyer, but there will be no weapons on it if that's what you're interested in."

Francis scowled. A large reason why his superiors had approved the treaty was the opportunity of advanced weaponry which King James could use to squash an increasing anti-Catholic sentiment in Great Britain and Europe. Personally, Francis couldn't wait to be commended for properly facilitating a profitable alliance and be sent back home to Surrey where a certain handsome, strapping, son of a baker used to live just down the street. Alas, it would appear as if the Governor would be stuck in the infernal New World with his insatiable wife for a bit longer.

"Then, pray tell, what shall be on this flyer?"

"Fuzi. About two billion of it."

Francis couldn't believe his ears, "Maybe I'm mishearing you, Fuzi? I mean no offense, but Fuzi is not a recognized currency."

"Not yet. If Britain expects to form a functional relationship with Cahokia, we'll need to be able to speak the same economical tongue."

"But already the rest of the world exchanges in gold or silver! Wouldn't it be easier to acclimate to them instead of forcing everyone else to adjust to you?"

"These are Cahokia's terms. The people here have never understood the obsession with gold or silver. Why would they? It's too soft to make tools and difficult to produce."

Francis was awestruck. Never in his life had it occurred to him that gold and silver could be deemed worthless. Why would it have? Everybody around him, his government, his subjects, his family, all yearned for the shiny useless metals. He mustered, "King James shall not be pleased."

"Tell King James that if he wants his medicine, his bisoons, his flyers, he must accept our generous gift of two billion Fuzi. You'll still be able to use your precious gold and silver, just not to buy from Cahokia. We only accept Fuzi."

Diane finished her drink, sifting the liquid between her teeth. This was a crucial step, getting Britain hooked on Fuzi. True, it currently had no value anywhere else than Cahokia, but once the rest of the world realized they could purchase superior technology with Fuzi, then they would clamor for it and its value would shoot up. An added bonus was a quick solution to Cahokia's inflation problems.

Francis drooped, "England needs Cahokia's support..."

"No weapons of any kind will be shipped to you. Cahokia is not in the war profiteering business. We're a neutral third party, and it's going to stay that way," Diane basked in his groveling, sipping her drink without a hint of urgency, "Your king has nothing to fear. In the next twenty-four months, England's economy will outpace even the Dutch. His contingency will be too busy ushering in a new epoch to care about whether their monarch is a Catholic or a Protestant."

The Governor had no more firm ground to stand on. Diane gulped down the rest of her glass and left to go attend the festivities, leaving the Governor to stew.

Diane threaded her way through the crowd, greeted people, and sampled food from different booths. She competed in an axe throwing competition, which she lost horribly to a group of shit-talking Apache.

She approached a group of black slaves running a booth selling pies and purchased one. The man who took her money was jolted when she asked, "What's your name?"

"Isaac, ma'am."

"Having fun, Isaac?"

"Of course, ma'am." Isaac was unhealthily skinny with a greying ring of hair.

"Where are you from?"

"Grace plantation, outside of Yorktown."

"You like it here in Cahokia?"

"Course, it's quite different, but I do enjoy it," Isaac bobbed his head. Diane loved his voice, a syrupy mixture of African and British. "And Yorktown? You like it there as well?"

Isaac scrunched his eyes. He quickly nodded, "Yorktown is my home. You know what they say, there ain't no place like home."

"If you had to change one thing about it, what would you change?"

"Nothing, ma'am, nothing at all. It's the picture of per-
fection."

"Really?"

Isaac stared at her for a flustered moment before shaking his head furiously, "Here's your pie, ma'am. Better eat it
before it goes cold."

She noticed a group of prim white men glancing and tut-
ting at her disapprovingly.

"What's your real name?"

"My god-given name is Isaac..."

"What about your parents, Isaac? Were they named by
God?"

Isaac shoved the packaged pie into Diane's hands and
backed away. One of the Englishmen started towards the
booth. Hatha appeared by Diane's elbow and led her away
quickly. Diane looked back to see Isaac being viciously be-
rated. She ripped her arm from Hatha's grip and began
marching back towards the booth. Hatha grabbed her once
more, "Come, it's an emergency!"

"Give me one second!"

"Diane! They're here! The Europeans..."

"They're here? What do you mean *here*?"

"Coastal sentries spotted them. They're probably a hundred miles off shore."

Diane and Hatha rushed away to an awaiting bisoon.
Hatha kicked it into gear and sped east towards the coast.
She dialed Chaska who picked up immediately, "We're on it,
aquatic blockade is ready."

"Good. How many?"

"A thousand, maybe more."

Diane quivered in excitement, "Find out the exact number. As long as it doesn't exceed two thousand, we'll be fine. I'm set to arrive in-" She checked a paper map and did a quick calculation, "three hours. That gives me plenty of time."

"Uhhhh, I don't think so," Chaska replied, "We did a fly over and they're moving a lot faster than you told us they would. It's very odd."

"How so?"

"Their ships have sails but our barometers aren't showing a strong tailwind. Some of the ships haven't even unfurled their sail, but they're still moving."

"They must be rowing then."

"We didn't see any. Could there be another way they're powering their ships?"

Hatha pumped the gas, zigzagging between orange and red sassafras trees. There was only one possibility to how Europeans had been able to install boat motors to an entire fleet. It couldn't have gone through the British, as they were on the brink of war with the rest of Europe. The French and the Spanish couldn't have gotten their hands on a bisoon or helicopter motor through their colonies because none had fallen to the Europeans' inferior tactics. A tight inventory of each vehicle was kept before and after each conflict. There was only one possibility - somebody had given them the technology for a whale-oil powered engine and they had modified it for their ships. Diane knew who the culprit was. If he had given them the ability to cross the Atlantic with the heat of internal combustion engines, what else had he taught them to do? Diane started to feel nauseous. Maybe the Europeans weren't just going to roll over.

Rokel was a huge man, his biceps thicker than the waist of a small child. His black skin glistened with sweat underneath a fitted British navy uniform. Rokel was definitely not part of the British navy, but he wore the uniform to make his clients feel more at home. Keeping the books for the world's largest slave port wasn't an easy job. Naimbanna, the Obai or King of Koya, had elected Rokel to run the massive corporation. He had studied in England, and thus spoke the simple language better than most Englishmen. Rokel not only kept record of hundreds of thousands of humans being loaded on to British, French, Portuguese, and Dutch ships, but also the imports that were coming off of these ships.

The most important import was weaponry. The Obai had explained it as such: Europeans needed slaves for God knows what, free labor, human meat, it didn't really matter. These crazed white men were willing to give guns, ammunition, alcohol, textiles, and factory-made goods in exchange for slaves, an abundant resource for the Kingdom of Koya. European ships would arrive, offload these products which Rokel and his staff would count and record carefully. Then they would fill the same ships with already enslaved people, criminals, and citizens of neighboring enemies. The guns and ammunition were then used to expand the Kingdom of Koya as well as capture more slaves, in turn increasing demand.

Rokel had done such a good job at growing margins that the Obai had honored him with the title of Gbana, the Temne equivalent of a noble. Rokel's thirty plus years of experience left him feeling collected most of the time. This was not one of those times. Two foreigners had requested passage to Jamestown on the next departing slaver. These two, an Oriental woman and an Arab man, were asking for a ride across the ocean on a boat that wasn't a slaver. They stood timidly in front of the frazzled Rokel, who scribbled away while he yelled at them in French, "You hitch a ride on any ship leaving my harbor, you're on a slaver. There are no other options!"

José was green. Before fighting their way up the ranks to Rokel, they had witnessed the atrocities of Koya's slave port. Hundreds of poor souls loaded onto boats, often wailing in terror. Children forcibly separated from their mothers and father and whipped into compliance. The smell drove José mad, and he couldn't imagine spending weeks on end with this in the middle of the ocean.

"There's no fishing boats or ferries?" he asked. Rokel scoffed and went back to his furious calculations. Li Mei pulled José to the side and hissed, "What's the problem?"

"I don't want to go on a slave ship!"

"Why not? You don't have slaves in your time?"

"No! Well, not where I lived."

"Well, you're in this time, so act like it." Li Mei spun them around to face Rokel, who didn't look up from his books. She cleared her throat, "We'll be fine on a slaver. When's the next boat we can go on?"

"Three days from now. You bring your own food and water. Koya is not responsible for any harm or death that occurs! Any rebellions or outbreaks are the crew's problem, not mine, understand?"

The two nodded. Rokel put down his quill and massaged his hands, taking in the odd couple.

"Tell me, why are you seeking passage on my ships? Why not depart from Portugal? You can buy or work your way across in much better conditions. You're not Cahokians, are you?"

José shook his head furiously, "God no!"

"We're searching for our brother," Li Mei chimed in, "He was sent to the Virginia Company as an indentured servant. He was supposed to come join us down in São Tomé after he paid off his time, but it's been long overdue. For the sake of urgency, we decided it would be quicker to cross here rather than spend additional months traveling north."

"I know for a fact that the VOC offers passage to Europe from São Tomé, why didn't you take that?" retorted Rokel, crossing his arms. Li Mei didn't miss a beat, "You haven't heard? Immigration from all European states are closed except to and from Britain. We thought that going up the Slave Coast on foot and then crossing over to Virginia would be quicker than going back up all the way to England."

"The VOC could have picked you up and taken you directly to Guyana?" Rokel knew the ways across the Atlantic better than anybody. Li Mei grinned, "Guyana doesn't exist anymore. Cahokia ran them out."

The slave accountant gazed silently at Li Mei, then, in rapid-fire Portuguese, he cried, "You're too well connected to have been living in São Tomé! Meet my assistant, Kisi, on dock number seven three days from now. It'll depart before the sun rises. Now leave me."

"*Obrigado*," replied Li Mei. José repeated the phrase before they scuttled out. Rokel stroked his chin then called in Pasande, a middle aged man who resembled a praying mantis.

"Fetch me the wanted papers from Portugal and the VOC. France's as well."

For the next three days, Li Mei and José scrambled to collect enough food and water for the several-month-long voyage. They spent every last cent they had. Even though José protested wildly, Li Mei spent the first night with a rich merchant, letting José sneak into the house at night to raid the merchant's treasures, which the pair sold off in the nearby market for as much salted food and barrels of fresh water as they could. José couldn't stop thinking about how easy it would have been to cross if they had his plane and it still worked.

In the late evening of the second night, Rokel was where he usually was, sitting at his desk nose deep in his books. Pasande entered with a stack of wanted papers and plopped them down on the corner of Rokel's desk.

"What in the hell are these? Get them off my desk!"

"Those are the felony descriptions you asked for!" Pasande wandered out. Rokel looked at them, reached for it, but then decided that the imbalance of Susu slaves over Fuba slaves was a more pressing issue than a couple of foreign criminals. He'd check later in the night.

Around midnight, Li Mei and José arrived at dock number seven, dragging their cargo. Kisi, an unenthusiastic dockhand, looked at them blankly when they recounted what Rokel had supposedly instructed them to do. He responded, "Rokel told me nothing of the sort."

"Go ask him yourself!"

"I can't, I'm in charge of loading up this ship." Kisi pointed to a group of angry Englishmen pushing a huddled cluster of naked, chained Africans onto the boat. José shuddered.

"They look like they're handling it pretty well," Li Mei suggested, "We'll load on our cargo, go see Rokel and get confirmation. If he says no, kick us off and keep our cargo on board."

Kisi jogged towards Rokel's fortress. It was hotly debated throughout the slave market about how Rokel managed to work so much and sleep so little, while maintaining pristine records. Only a select few knew that the answer was a strong stimulant from a South American leaf.

Kisi had the luck of walking in on one of Rokel's stimulant consumption breaks. The record keeper was crushing up a pile of leaves in a tiny stone mortar and pestle, then smearing it over his gums. Rokel yelled, "What do you want!?"

"Sorry, sir. Two mzungus claim you authorized their passage on the Charleston ship?"

"Yes, yes! Let them board. Go away!"

Once Kisi had gone, Rokel pasted the rest of coca ooze on his gums and and noticed the pile of still unread wanted descriptions that Pasande had delivered earlier. Curiosity got the best of him so he shuffled through them to see if there could be any potential reward money for the two mzungus.

José and Li Mei lugged the last of their supplies into an aft compartment of the boat. Slaves were still being loaded up a rickety gangplank, black and white crew men rushing them on with shouts and cracks of the whip. Li Mei watched in interest, while José stared out at the Atlantic, trying his best not to vomit.

Meanwhile in Rokel's office, the coked-up record keeper had found a fresh wanted description from the VOC that described José and Li Mei with vivid accuracy. The reward was 10,000 guilders. Rokel attempted to rise, but his legs had fallen asleep due to consecutive hours of unuse. His chair tipped backwards and he sprawled out on the floor, slamming the back of his head hard on the stone back wall. Rokel moaned, dizzy.

Onboard the *Charleston*, the last of the slaves were being secured below decks. The crew readied the boat for embarkation, yanking an uncountable number of ropes this way and that, taking inventory, and yelling at each other.

"I don't think I can do this..." José mumbled to Li Mei. She patted him on the back, "You have to." The captain, a bearded Scot, took his place at the helm. José's hand found Li Mei's and squeezed hard. A frizzy-haired Angolan sailor shouted up to the Captain in English, "One minute, Capn', a couple of bodies we need to discard."

"On the double!" screeched back the Captain. A few crew-mates disappeared into the lower deck. They appeared minutes later, carrying a large tarp on which five or so unmoving slaves lay. The men waddled this tarp over towards the side of the ship and set it down on the edge. Then they moved to the inner side of the tarp and lifted. One of the slaves, a particularly bony old woman, opened her eyes and then her mouth in a silent scream. Without hesitation, the crew hoisted the tarp so the bodies, including the still breathing woman, tumbled into the rocky cove. José watched as a few bubbles escaped to the surface.

In his office, Rokel came to, pulling himself up. The back of his head was throbbing and he felt woozy, but the thought of 10,000 guilders numbed the pain just enough to stumble out of the building towards the docks.

The sun began to rise, giant rays of glorious light bursting from the dark forbidding ocean. José hoped and almost expected to see Cahokia outlined by the solar pillars, but he saw nothing but a flat line. The crew untied the mooring lines, allowing the receding tide to pull the boat out to sea. José puked.

Just as the boat's nose had rotated westward, Rokel's booming shouts echoed throughout the early morning. "Oh, fuck..." José rose, ready for action. Li Mei pulled him down quickly. The record keeper was sprinting towards the Charleston, waving a sheet of paper wildly.

Time slowed down as Li Mei watched some of the crew crane to hear Rokel. The Captain, who was enthralled in an argument with his first mate about latitudes, glanced over to land. Li Mei quickly extracted the sling, grabbed the nearest hard thing that was small enough to fit in the sling, an apple, and flung it with magnificent speed at the record keeper. The fruit exploded over the right side of Rokel's cranium, knocking him out cold. His huge frame collapsed onto the ground.

Li Mei tucked the sling into her pants and squatted down next to José. Several dock men approached Rokel's limp form and the Charleston's crew peered over in wonder at the commotion. Soon the Captain shouted at them to get back to their posts. The wails from a malnourished slave baby prompted a rather nasty looking Brit to run down below deck, unfurling a whip. José stared at the cavernous entrance to hell and said to Li Mei quietly, "I almost wish he had stopped us."

-

November, 1685

A thousand and fifty-seven large naval ships, mostly Dutch, French, and Spanish, churned towards the eastern seaboard. On one of these boats, Dewitt, wearing a leather eyepatch, stood on the deck, contemplating their chances of success. It had been an immense struggle to mobilize this many crews, along with outfitting each ship with an aquatic motor, the results of Vincenzo's genius. The Tuscan polymath had been able to redesign the plane's motor for water travel, after discovering that a durable plastic shell could be forged from melted cow horn.

This valiant undertaking had necessitated the formation of a new company, the Coalition of the Righteous. Credit had been available to every European state, except Great Britain who was considered an ally of Cahokia. The biggest donors were the Catholic and Protestant churches, a rare alliance that drove millions to invest in the ordained crusade, along with the added promise of unimaginable riches. All other European colonies had caught word of the ensuing opportunity and sent support.

Even with the largest military force the world had ever seen, Dewitt still felt unprepared. The only notable technological advancement that they had on their side were the motors. Dewitt had cleverly placed a Silbo whistle speaker on each ship, allowing complex messages to be passed rapidly over great distances, but what was that compared to radios?

"Tell them to turn five degrees south," Dewitt instructed a small, ratty Spaniard. The Canary Island native faced the rest of the boats and whistled sharply, relaying the direction to thousands of other Silbo speakers on each other ship. Soon everyone was turning five degrees south.

On shore, Diane lowered a pair of binoculars. She sat in the middle of a round booth with a semi-circular panel covered by a sea of buttons and levers. This was the control booth from which Diane would conduct battle. Behind her, hundreds of Cahokian soldiers waited silently, watching the endless line of ships grow closer. They shifted nervously. Diane had made it clear that they were only there if the aquatic blockage failed. Chaska buzzed on the radio, "They're in range."

"Copy," Diane typed in an access code to the central keyboard. The control panel hummed to life. She could feel the eyes of her compatriots on her back.

"Tell them to load the guns!" Dewitt yelled to his Silbo whistler. The man began hastily whistling out the order when the ship shook unnaturally. The crew moved to the edge to see if they had struck a reef. Every other ship around them was shaking in the same fashion. Manuel swung down from the crow's nest, landing nimbly at Dewitt's side, "It can't be that shallow..."

The wooden hull creaked and both men could feel their ride start to slow. All the other boats were gradually losing speed, their crews running around at furious commands from captains and first mates. Not one ship could find a problem with the sails or the motors. After a minute, the entire fleet of the Coalition of the Righteous had come to a complete halt. The air was filled with motors being revved, sails being luffed, and Silbo being whistled.

"It's them," muttered Dewitt. Manuel squinted at the coastline.

"How?"

"A giant net, perhaps?"

Already hundreds of men were leaping into the frigid waters of the Atlantic, trying to see what exactly had stopped their progress. A shivering Greek was pulled onto their deck and towards Dewitt. With most of the crew crowding around, the Grecian sailor stuttered out, "No net, no net! I...I..."

"Out with it!" demanded Dewitt. The man was having a hard time describing something he didn't comprehend, "Some machine, with many tails. It's locked to the bottom of the ship! Every one!"

"Every one?!"

"Every ship! There's one on every ship. The tails swim east."

All eyes turned to Dewitt. He huffed his chest out, "What are you waiting for? Get it off!"

A deluge of men dove into the icy sea with ropes and blades. They hacked and pried but not a single ship was able to rid themselves of the ominous mechanical parasites. After an hour of hopeless toil, most had given up and ordered their men to return. Dewitt estimated that they were only a mile or two offshore, "To the tenders! We'll take them by land!"

"There's only enough room for fifteen, twenty maximum at a time. Most ships only have two or three tenders..." said Manuel doubtfully as the whistles of Silbo went up through the fleet. Dewitt produced a pistol and a brush snake, "Even still, that gives us a sizable army."

From her control booth, Diane spoke into her inner ear walkie to Chaska, "They're coming to you. Ready?"

"Only if you are."

"I won't wish you good luck, you don't need it."

The COR mercenaries steadily neared the shore, their tiny rowboats peppering the frothy water from either end of the horizon. Although the Cahokians had been assured many times the advantage tipped vastly towards them, it was difficult to visualize a victory over such a large army. Diane nudged a lever that activated smoke bombs to go off all around the Cahokian battalion, who took this as a sign to put on their infrared goggles. Cries of alarm went up all along the tenders for every COR soldier had lost sight of the enemy.

The first of the tenders touched the gravelly beach and thousands of mercenaries panicked. With no other recourse, they begin firing their muskets and pistols blindly into the fog. Each Cahokian had donned full body protective armor, so most of the bullets ricocheted off harmlessly, but the overwhelming amount of fire at one time dropped a few scores on the defending side. Enraged, the Cahokians retaliated.

The barrage lasted mere minutes. Diane watched in sick fascination as her troops massacred the COR soldiers with deadly precision. With their infrared goggles and assisted scopes, one Cahokian had the ability to take out at least five COR men without breaking a sweat. There was a mad scramble to jump back into the tenders and retreat. Diane commanded her soldiers through the radio, "Cease fire! Let them get back to their boats."

Manuel's spyglass fell to the floor, the four rounded glasses inside shattered on impact. He turned to the lanky Dutchman, his oldest friend, "You've led us in the mouth of the beast! Let us raise the white flag, at least we can save some lives!"

The one thing in the world that Dewitt could not stand was losing money on a venture. And he was on the verge of losing everything.

"Please, Dewitt! Salvage what you can! Please!"

The eyes of the entire crew fell upon Dewitt. He wanted nothing more to order more men into the tenders, but he could tell that a mutiny was close at hand. Dewitt dipped his head almost imperceptibly and a sigh of relief washed over the men. Once more, whistles rang through the air and white flags appeared above each deck.

In her booth, Diane leaned back, arching her back which was sore from sitting for too long. She pressed another button. A small drone launched into the air from a side compartment to her left and raced towards the disabled fleet.

The drone hovered along the ships, relaying a live feed to a screen in front of Diane. Eventually, she found Dewitt's boat and lowered the drone close enough to broadcast audio clearly to those below.

"Welcome back to Cahokia, Dewitt," Diane proclaimed smugly, "although, I wish it was under better pretenses."

Dewitt glared up at the humming sprite, "Too timid to negotiate with me in person?"

"That was quite foolish, ordering your men to come ashore with such hostility. Your investors will not be happy."

Dewitt scoffed, "What are your demands?"

"Two options. One, you tack eastward, return home, and all will be forgotten. Two, you come ashore, as friends, and sign a treaty. Both allow you to live. There's no wrong answer."

A few hundred tenders were just arriving back to the fleet. Dewitt watched as the bleeding, dying men were corralled back onto any ship that would take them.

"We can't turn back, we only have enough food and fresh water for a one-way trip."

"Then you choose the second option?"

Dewitt spit on the salt stained deck, "How can I be sure you shan't demolish the rest of us like you did my infantrymen?"

"I'll give you half an hour to discuss. In the meantime, enjoy Jean-Baptiste Lully."

French chamber music from the drone played out tauntingly. The ships' underwater attachments sank and rose in time with the tempo, alternating up, down, up, down so that the entire fleet had no choice but to hold on as they performed a dizzying waltz. Thousands upon thousands of sailors and mercenaries watched this horrifying display of Cahokian omnipotence. Some unseen deity could speak to them from the sky and move them around like they were toy boats in a bathtub.

Dewitt's mind raced for a solution to save not only his empire, but also his reputation.

"We're dealing with a force beyond our realm of understanding. Surrender, Dewitt. Our army bobs up and down to Louis' favorite composer. Let us go to shore, sign the damn treaty, escape with our own heads" begged the Angolan ex-pirate.

Dewitt turned towards the drone and beckoned it closer. The music instantly stopped, the fleet fell still, and the drone dropped down to a few feet above eye level.

"What are the terms of your proposed treaty?"

"This is only a financial agreement to hammer out trade between our parties. Cahokia wishes to trade with Europe and its colonies dearly but we are unaccustomed to your currencies. This treaty would require all exports out of Cahokia to be paid with Fuzi."

"But no one outside of Cahokia uses that?!" cried Dewitt.

The drone buzzed back, "The British now do. The second part of the treaty will generously award two and half billion Fuzi to the VOC. Not only are we letting you go, we're making you rich!"

"I realize what you're doing..." Dewitt clenched his fists. The drone fell slightly nearer to the seething Dutchman.

"Sorry, I didn't catch that? You have to speak towards the drone."

The rest of the COR men began shouting at Dewitt to take the deal, sign the treaty, and accept the gift. Dewitt's giant ego swelled against the tide, his mind shutting out their pleas. The clicks of pistols cocking meant nothing to him.

Diane's silky voice went on, "You're out of time, Commander. What will it be?"

Manuel recognized Dewitt's resolve, sprinted towards the edge of the deck, and chucked himself into the frigid Atlantic.

"I'm not the one who's out of time, Diane," Dewitt drew himself to his full height and stared defiantly into the lens of the drone.

"That was a mistake."

The little mechanical bug zoomed upwards. Dewitt took one last breath, savoring the scent of salt and gunpowder. Underneath their ship, the attached underwater propeller received a signal from land and ignited a condensed tank of nitroglycerin.

Even Diane was surprised by the size of the explosion. Screams from the rest of the boats along with hysteric whistling underscored the fire power that lay beneath each boat. Her shaking hand found a knob that triggered the rest of the fleet to swiftly pull ashore. Chaska appeared behind her, "Did you mean to do that?"

Diane stayed still, fixated on the fizzing, smoldering patch of ocean where Dewitt's boat once was. Chaska touched her tenderly on the shoulder, "What should we do with them?"

"Feed them, tend to their wounded. They'll sign the damn thing."

After the last ship was beached, the hundreds of thousands of COR mercenaries ate a meal of grilled potatoes and corn on the cob. All felt dumbfounded by the queer nature of their captors and by the speed of which the Cahokians had been able to scrape together enough food for so many. Many refused to eat. Diane, Chaska, Nikan, and the Cahokian soldiers watched from the side, discussing in Sauk how to proceed. Nobody noticed Manuel scuttle up the beach and into the protection of a rocky estuary.

-

CHAPTER

24

January, 1686

Weeks after weeks of witnessing the most inhuman conditions imaginable left its scar on José, but what really tormented him was the fact that he was just a witness, a passenger, a spectator. What would happen to the minds of the enslaved men, women, and children?

Li Mei fared better, as slavery had been a common occurrence during her time, but the constant smell of festering feces and rotting flesh drove her mad. The pair found solace only in each other's company, often swapping stories about their own times. Li Mei refused to share too much from her time, but she gave José the impression that 1730s were a turbulent, technological advanced era. She gave him snippets of a world full of automation, medical wonders, and cyber conformity.

As time went on, José found that he had forgotten a scarily large portion of his life before the chronological transference. Many nights he gazed up at the stars and quizzed himself on different details of his life in Capron. Sarah and Kyle Peterson were less than insignificant. Instead, Noemi dominated his dreams and fantasies, her emerald eyes and porcelain skin flashing just out of reach. The only person who he really wanted to see again from Capron was his father.

The slaver's crew had just done their daily corpse dump and were just starting to whip several naked men to dance in the middle of the deck, when one salty Irishman manning the crow's nest pronounced, "Land ho!" and pointed to a thin sliver of brown on the horizon.

Li Mei and José embraced tightly, tears pouring down their mushed-together faces. About two weeks into the trip, Li Mei had caught José tottering on the boat's edge. She had pulled him down and comforted him as he sobbed and whispered propositions of a slave rebellion. She quickly and firmly admonished this idea.

Their boat, the *Charleston*, was named not for any wealthy benefactor or royalty, but for its native city, Charleston, Province of Carolina, which happened to be their current destination.

Dockhands rushed around to receive the arriving slaver. José and Li Mei clutched each other tightly. The two had run out of food three days prior.

Before any member of the *Charleston* had a chance to debark, four metal planks clanked down on the deck. Redcoats and Cahokian soldiers swarmed onto the deck. They didn't raise a weapon, but their formidable demeanor suggested sudden movements by the crew would be taken poorly. José hissed, "They're here for us!"

"Maybe," replied Li Mei, "Maybe not."

A large blond Redcoat swaggered onboard, shook hands gruffly with the Captain, and spoke loudly, "Welcome to Charleston. In the past, we'd receive you with enough sugar, cotton, and tobacco to knock out a Scot, but there's been a change in policy. You shall relinquish your human cargo for a total of-"

The man peeked a notepad, ran his finger along a line, and proclaimed, "fifty thousand Fuzi." This causes a sudden uproar from the crew of the *Charleston*, but several Cahokian soldiers cocked their automatic weapons and the protests diminished to a surly grumble. The large Redcoat clicked his tongue and his men began bringing Africans from below deck. He spotted José and Li Mei, both looking very out of place, and confronted them, "Members of the crew?"

"Passengers," corrected José. Li Mei smiled as sweetly as she could since she hardly understood English. The officer produced his little notepad once more, "Nation of origin?"

"Cahokia," José blurted, unable to think of a better answer.

"Haven't met many Cahoks who can converse in the King's English. What were you doing in Africa?"

"Governmental intel," José offered.

The officer scribbled this down, "Names?"

"I'm Seattle and this is Pocahontas. She doesn't speak English."

"Better English than my Sauk, I'm sure. All Cahoks have been granted indefinite visitor status in King James' colonies. Fuzi loans are in the city center. Welcome to Carolina." He moved off to attend to the mouthy Captain.

The Africans were filing down the gangplanks, shivering nakedly in the crisp autumn breeze. Dockhands ushered them towards a formidable brick building. José sidled up to a Redcoat and inquired politely, "What's going to happen to them?"

"The blacks? It's up to them, I suppose. New Royal decree, triangle trade is no more. We're givin' em the option to cross back or stay here as Cahoks. Thought you'd'a known that," the Brit hustled off.

José stood watching the parade of destitute souls trudge towards an uncertain fate. He felt a little better that they wouldn't be sold into slavery, but their treatment on the voyage here had been nothing short of infernal. José trusted Cahokia as far as he could spit, which wasn't far at all because he hadn't drunk freshwater in at least a day. Li Mei jumped up and down excitedly, pulling on José's shirt.

"Come on, let's find something to eat!"

Charleston had served as a port for slave trade for the past few decades, but now, with an influx of Cahokian technology and Fuzi, it was rapidly becoming one of the biggest commercial hubs on the Atlantic. A constant barrage of boats, planes, bisoons, electric motorcycles, and foot-travel stormed the city daily from every direction. Cahokians roamed freely and Sauk was just as common as English. José and Li Mei found their way into the city center where several booths were offering Fuzi loans.

"We shouldn't," Li Mei decided, "They'll know we're not Cahokian."

"So what?"

"We need to keep a low profile."

José's stomach audibly growled, "We need to eat, and stealing food will be the quickest way to blow cover."

"You speak Sauk?" retorted Li Mei.

José threw up his arms, "I'll go to a British one!"

Pretending to speak broken English, José approached the friendliest looking woman he could find who sat behind one of the loan booths. He charmed the woman with adorable linguistic blunders and a good deal of running his hands through his hair. In twenty minutes, José and Li Mei were contentedly vacuuming steaming porridge at a tavern down the road. José had finagled five hundred Fuzi with a one percent interest rate and a repayment date in a year. These loans were employed by the Cahokian economic bureau in order to circulate as much Fuzi into the British economy as possible.

They gobbled down a few thousand more calories, to the amusement of the other tavern patrons. After, they took to the streets to find a mode of transportation. Charleston had just recently installed solar-powered street-lamps on every corner and so crowds of onlookers flocked underneath them. Both José and Li Mei found this hilarious and spent a few minutes imitating the human moths. A gaggle

of Cahokian women passed, noticed José and Li Mei imitating the dumbfounded Europeans, and joined in, chattering in Sauk. Evidently, street lamps were old news for
Cahokians.

A great many vehicles whizzed by, including a large
green bisoon. José marveled, "They have cars, now!"

"Cars?" asked Li Mei.

"That moving thing with wheels? You don't call it a car?"

"Cahokians called them bisoons. Probably our best bet."

A hoard of school boys ran past them towards a growing
crowd. José and Li Mei wandered over to the edge of the
mob and stood on their tippy toes. It turned out to be an
unveiling of a new product - an energy cooker, a metal box
roughly a foot in all dimensions, a glass door on the front, a
series of buttons on the side. A fat man with mutton chops
was preaching about this wonder of the world, conducting
his verbose narration with a frozen piglet leg.

"Since Our Lord banished Adam and Eve from the Garden Eden, folk have been using fire and water to prepare
meals. God hath seen fit to ordain us with a gift, a gift of
speed, NAY, the ability to harness his holy spirit's energy
in order to properly nourish ourselves! Observe this frozen
leg of a swine, colder than Peter the Great's beloved!"

The people responded well to this jab. José leaned in to
Li Mei, "It's just a microwave?"

"Why do you call it that?" hissed back Li Mei.

José was stumped. Did he forget or did he ever know?

"I shall place the limb into the receptacle," continued
Mutton Chops, popping the door open, garnering some

oohs and *aahs,* "Once inside, we must summon the glory of the almighty, simply by punching in six buttons in order to receive the divine gift. You sir, how long does it take you to roast a swine limb?"

A crippled Cornish blacksmith shouted drunkenly, "Half the life of a dog, I reckon!"

That got an even bigger reaction, so Mutton Chops placed the piglet leg into the energy cooker, swung the door shut, fingered the buttons, and the machine came to life. In the front, a woman fainted. All grew wide eyed; a hush fell. José wanted to yell, "Just wait till they invent hot pockets!" but he thought better of it.

"Just three minutes, mes gens, and then, after a prayer, we feast!"

In his old life, José would have compulsively scrolled on his phone while waiting for a microwave to finish, but now the rotating hock of meat behind the glass hypnotized him. This energy cooker reminded him of home, of the afternoon snacks he would make before Angel came home from work, of the time Bernie tried to make EasyMac without any water, and of course his aunt Cindy who would always microwave a mug of water for tea instead of boiling it.

"You're crying?" Li Mei watched a tear roll down his cheek. José shook his head furiously, "It's fucking hilarious!"

After the energy cooker dinged, the crowd leaned forward in anticipation. Mutton Chops popped open the hatch. The steaming pig leg sat there, ready for consumption. "Who would like a taste of heaven?"

José and Li Mei abandoned the presentation. They needed a place to rest, having slept on the hard wood for too long. If José had taken the time to scan the crowd, he would have noticed a man who resembled Dion Sanders. However, he didn't, but Manuel did see him. The Angolan ex-pirate, now ex-mercenary, inconspicuously melted away from the crowd and stealthily pursued his old co-pilot.

The next day, José and Li Mei slept well into the afternoon, catching up on months of sleep deprivation. Even Li Mei's tremendous snoring wasn't able to shake José from his slumber, but it did wake a group of Danish fishermen who thought a flyer was using the next room as a runway.

Feeling refreshed, the two set out to find a bisoon. José asked around, learning that bisoons weren't yet available for regular citizens. One person suggested he try a motorbike, which could be bought for a thousand Fuzi. Li Mei and José only had around four hundred Fuzi left between the two of them, and a motorbike could only seat one person safely.

José and Li Mei went back to the city center in order to get another loan from a different booth, this one had slightly worse interest rates and a much sooner repayment date, but debt wasn't high on their list of concerns. All the while, Manuel stalked from a distance.

-

CHAPTER

25

December, 1699

Although Diane had been able to advance the humanity hundreds of years into the future in under two decades, culture was still archaic. Everything had to be framed in terms of the hyper-zealous religions that dominated practically every aspect of society. The energy cooker didn't cook with electromagnetic radiation, it baked by the grace of God. Factories and transportation weren't gifts from an avid time-traveling physicist, but a present from the Great Spirit.

When Diane brought the twenty-second century back to 1685, the biggest risk she took was believing this process could and would happen on a short time scale. Her hypothesis predicted that the late seventeenth and eighteenth centuries would also be able to cope with accelerating growth. In her original timeline, atheism and agnosticism had taken root for a sufficient percentage of the population that science became revered, whereas at the end of the seventeenth century, theism remained mandatory. Much to Diane's relief, this didn't stunt efficient progress. Her own early struggles with Cahokian shamans had concerned her, but it was human nature to advance, so religion conformed to technology just as technology conformed to religion.

In the grand scheme of things, a few centuries difference was nothing at all. Everything she had done and would do, would eventually come to pass one way or the other.

Even though her plan seemed ahead of schedule, Diane was far from content. Those she killed, Dewitt, his crew, Zula, and Askook haunted her. She could only sleep by thinking of the hundreds of millions of souls she had supposedly saved from colonialism, slavery, wars, and disease.

Diane thumbed her way through a schematics' manual. She was on a private jet on its way to Tenochtitlan, once a great Aztec city, now the largest military base in the Cahokian Empire. It served as an ideal location for commerce and travel, smack dab in the middle of North and South Cahokia.

They were just a week away from the dawn of a new century. Cahokia's influence had spread to every corner of the world, facilitated by the international spread of Fuzi.

The schematics' manual that Diane revised contained plans for a special weapon. It wasn't the most modern tech that Diane had introduced. Scientists around the world worshipped Diane's two zettabytes of scientific records. The Cahokian space program was in full swing, already three satellites had been launched and a manned mission was in the works. Many societies leapt from carbon power to nuclear. Electricity was almost ubiquitous. Everything electrical came out of Cahokia, loaded with Cahokian software. Even computers were popping up on most continents. Smartphones would have to wait until there were enough satellites to form a network, but it was just around the corner. All of this could be rendered useless if this particular weapon got in the wrong hands, which is why there existed only one copy of its schematics, the one currently in Diane's hands.

The onboard washroom door opened, Manuel stepped out and took the seat next to Diane. Roughly thirteen years prior, the Angolan mercenary had become Diane's chief advisor, a role in which he thrived. Obviously, Diane was at first quite reluctant to take on Dewitt's ex-first-mate, but after lengthy interrogations and lie-detector tests, he had proved a worthy right-hand and especially valuable in dealing with foreign nations. In his escapades as a pirate and with the VOC, Manuel could inform Diane about any country in the Eastern hemisphere. His intel had helped Cahokian expansion, and Manuel was compensated. What really made him trustworthy in her eyes was the fact that he had reported tailing José.

He had claimed that the renegade and a mysterious woman left Charleston in the autumn of 1685. They had been heading towards Cahokia city, but Manuel lost track of them on the way. Diane had deployed teams of soldiers and drones to investigate the entire continent, but in the last thirteen years, José and his enigmatic companion were nowhere to be found.

"Manu, you ever wonder what happened to José?" chided Diane, closing the schematics' booklet. Manuel shrugged, "All the time. Perhaps he realized coming here was a mistake."

"A mistake of what?" Diane pondered out loud, "He was coming to talk to me or he was coming to kill me. He must have gotten cold feet or something happened to him..."

"Ready for the presentation?"

"Of course, I can't imagine it going badly," snorted Diane, "They're going to shit blood."

A few hours later, their plane landed at one of the many Tenochtitlan base runways, the tarmac wet from a light drizzle. Diane and Manuel quickly moved into a bisoon, which drove itself towards the testing site. The self-driving bisoon stopped at three different stops, each time Diane rolled down the window to confirm their identity and clearance level to a posted sentry. After the third checkpoint, their bisoon skidded toward a towering metal hangar sitting on the top of a small barren plateau. Their vehicle zipped into the only entrance, just large enough to fit the bisoon. An automatic door rolled down, sealing the building.

Inside, a small gathering of high-ranking Cahokian officials gathered around the bisoon. Nikan, sporting grey hair and presidential garb, helped Diane out. Nikan had become the de facto president of Cahokia, at least in title. Diane still ruled from behind the curtain. In 1687, the High Council had been coerced into amending the constitution, giving a majority portion of their political sway to the State Secretary.

"You're late," Nikan teased, "I was running out of stories of the old days."

"Please, find a seat," Diane gestured to an array of plastic chairs over to the side, and people rushed to sit, excited for the show to start. Manuel went over to stand next to the door they had entered through. Diane placed herself in front of the attendees, feeling their energy, building suspense.

"I asked you here today because you are the lucky few who will get to witness the very thing that will solidify Pax Cahokia. You are also the lucky few who will ever know about this, because it shall remain a secret to the public for as long as I live."

She nodded to Manuel who pressed a button on the wall, which opened the door. In drove another bisoon, this one driven by two Cahokian soldiers in head-to-toe body arm. The new six-wheeled vehicle parked next to Diane. The two soldiers hopped out and began unloading various electronic devices from the back, laying them out a few feet apart in a semi-circle on the other side of Diane near the middle of the hangar. Each one was connected to its own battery pack.

"These two warriors are members of a special ops force which has been training rigorously for the past three years," Diane nodded to them, and they bobbed their helmets back, "We're keeping their identity hidden for their own safety."

The two soldiers switched on each device, an energy cooker, a washing machine, a desktop computer, and so on. Once they turned the last one on, they stood next to Manuel over on the side. The spectators shifted nervously.

Manuel strode over to the soldiers' bisoon's trunk, extracted what looked like a rifle with a rotund cone on the end, and handed it to Diane delicately.

"This is an Electromagnetic Pulse Ray Gun," Diane hefted it up to show off the shiny, smooth exterior, "When fired, it releases a controlled transient electromagnetic disturbance. It's silent, invisible, scentless, holds hours and hours of charge. Fire it at a person and nothing will happen. I doubt they would feel anything. When it's fired at electrical equipment..."

Diane pointed the ray gun at the energy cooker, yanking on the trigger. The purring microwave shut off. Diane blasted the devices one by one, each losing power. Manuel pressed his watch and the self-driving bisoon that Diane and he arrived in squealed to life, racing towards the other side of the hangar. Diane raised the ray gun, tutted, and took aim. The bisoon made a large curve, heading straight for the onlookers. Many jumped to their feet instinctively, ready to scatter out of the way. Diane nonchalantly fired and the bisoon died, losing all of its momentum and rolling to a stop several yards away from her guests. Stunned applause broke out.

"I don't have to explain to you all why this can only be held by Cahokian hands."

Diane handed the ray gun to one of the soldiers and spread her arms triumphantly, "Any questions?"

"Why doesn't your facial recognition software get past beards?" said the soldier holding the ray gun in plain American English. He fired the ray gun several times at Diane and into the audience, disabling any electronic devices on their persons. Manuel pulled a pistol from his waistband and steadied it on Diane, who was entirely focused on the soldier holding the ray gun.

"You..."

The soldier took off his helmet to reveal dark curly hair. The man was handsome, lithe, his angular face covered in a thick beard.

"Howdy."

Li Mei flung off her helmet, produced a pistol from a holster and leveled it on the crowd, who collectively gasped and cowered. She shouted in Sauk, "No sudden movements, and no one gets hurt! Contacting anybody is pointless, we've disabled all electronics."

"That goes for your ear radio as well," Manuel growled at Diane.

Li Mei and José quickly rounded all the officials up, bound and gagged them, and placed them on their stomachs in the middle of the hangar. Meanwhile, Manuel hoisted Diane into the passenger's seat of the bisoon that still had power, shutting the doors after he sat in the driver's seat.

"You lied to me for thirteen years?" sputtered Diane.

"With ease. I confronted José and his friend on our way to Cahokia City and I helped them change their identity. After I became your advisor, I guided them through the ranks of the military until they landed in the EMP unit."

"You've been planning on avenging Dewitt's death this entire time?!"

Manuel shook his head, "Dewitt was a means to an end. Just like I was to you, and you are now to us. No, we have a different motive."

José and Li Mei hopped into the backseat. Diane gave Li Mei a confused glare, "I don't know who you are, but you made a mistake getting roped in with these two."

"You don't know me yet, but you will," Li Mei replied snidely, then wagged her time travel device in Diane's face which turned white as a sheet.

"We'd know each other quite well in about three decades."

"Tell us how to work it," José snapped, "What do the symbols mean?"

Li Mei's time travel device's screen read "J10(23)".

"The amount of energy the device has charged. Joules by ten to the twenty third power."

Manuel prodded her with the butt of his pistol. "Show us how to activate it."

The trio watched carefully as Diane pressed a sequence of spots on the screen which lit up. A digital keypad appeared.

"You press the number of years you want to travel, then press the backwards or forwards button on the following screen to determine whether you want to go to the past or future."

"What about acceleration?" demanded José.

"It'll tell you the proper meters per second squared required. The farther you travel, the more acceleration you need."

"What is enough to get me back to 2019?"

Diane sighed, "If you remember so many years ago, even if you managed to activate the device, traveling to the future will only bring you to the future of this timeline, not the one we were born in. Everything you knew is gone."

"You're lying! Li Mei said that you know how to get me back!" cried José, looking at Li Mei for back up. His seasoned companion returned his gaze with sheepish deflation. The pilot felt his stomach tighten.

Le Mei swallowed, "I'm really sorry, José. I knew you would only help me if you thought there was a chance to go back home."

José was too stunned to feel angry. Tears cascaded down into his knotted beard, "Then why?"

"Yeah, why?" chided Diane childishly. Manuel cocked his pistol and fired a round point blank into the physicist's forehead. Blood, skull, and frontal cortex spattered over the passenger window.

"Manuel! What the fuck!?" screamed José. Manuel reached over, took the original time travel device out of Diane's breast pocket, opened the passenger door, and pushed Diane's corpse onto the ground, which landed with a splat. He closed the door again.

"She served her purpose."

"How about some fucking closure?!"

Manuel shook his head, "This is not a Greek tragedy. She got what she deserved."

"How the fuck are we going to get out of here? We just killed their goddamn messiah!"

"Relax," Li Mei tried to pat José on the back but he swatted it away. She held her hands up defensively, "We are members of the Cahokian military with high level clearance, remember? We'll be able to get far away long before anyone comes inside this level five restricted facility."

The three passed effortlessly through the three checkpoints and into the damp plains of central Cahokia. They drove and drove, trying to put as much distance between them and any sign of civilization. José wanted to kill them both. He ground his teeth, "For once, tell me the truth. Why did you do this?"

Manuel brought the bisoon to a halt. They were now in the middle of the desert. Li Mei explained calmly, "I brought the idea to Manuel and we debated telling you. My time, the 1730s, will be rife with corruption, privacy breaches, a single totalitarian government run by an omnipotent AI whose servers are controlled solely by Diane. We'd be more secure than safe, more exploited than valuable. You telling me all those stories about your native time on the slaver made me want to see what the world would be like without her."

"My world had Diane in it!"

"We want a world that doesn't get an injection of the future, a life that progresses naturally."

José scoffed, "Y'all are full of shit..."

"We're going to go back to 1681 and prevent Diane from meddling," concluded Li Mei.

"You can come with us or not, no hard feelings either way," added Manuel. José studied the two people who had replaced his parents. He pondered what could possibly lay in store for him in 1681.

"Fucking idiots..."

José swung open his door and jumped to the muddy ground. Manuel rolled down his window and tossed the original time travel device to José, who instinctively caught it. Manuel grinned, "Use it wisely."

He gunned the bisoon forward. Li Mei waved from the backseat. The vehicle sprinted across the prairie like a mechanical lion, growing smaller in the distance. José saw a flash of blue light, then a flash of green, and the sound of the engine ceased.

-

EPILOGUE

August, 1712

After Diane's assassination, citizens of the immense Cahokian Empire went on with their lives blissfully ignorant. Nikan led a frantic search for the missing bisoon and imposters, but they came up empty-handed.

Eventually, Nikan's lack of aggressive tactics allowed the High Council to re-seize control over Cahokia. Without a distinct idea of where to go next, technological growth slowed, but only slightly. Many nations and monarchs realized the financial potential of advancement so they invested deeply into it but in their own pious ways.

In the following decade, Cahokia tried its best to police the world. It stretched itself too thin, eventually splitting into factions that reflected the tribes of old. Hordes of Europeans, Asians, and Africans migrated to the Cahokia in order to get a slice of modern life, many bringing back what they obtained to their homelands.

In the summer of 1712, a lone cloaked figure trekked across the sunny, temperate coast of Northern Genoa. Ahead lay a village tucked into the rocky slope.

José paused at the precipice of a cliff, removed his hood, and examined a world map on which hundreds of marks showed where he had visited. A healthy moustache framed his strong, clean-cut chin, and his long hair was tied in back with a bit of twine. Despite being in his mid-forties, José exuded youth and agility, as one does when they spend their life exploring the world on foot. Since Diane's death, he had attempted to stay off the grid, which was becoming harder and harder, especially with the rise of personal computing.

Subsequent to Manuel and Li Mei's departure, José had set out to find the only thing in this world that could make him happy. After years of searching, José was close to giving up.

The village couldn't have been more than two hundred people. It only still existed as a vacation destination for several rich Spanish bankers, who employed a majority of the villagers in their opulent estates. José wandered into the closest watering hole.

"If you want a job, Emilio is the man you want to see," advised the bartender, pouring a glass of refreshing cider for the stranger, "He refuses to use robots, and for that, we thank God."

"He lives alone?"

"Him and his wife. And the help of course."

After numbing his sore feet with enough beer to black out a horse, José found his way towards the cliff-hanging villa just outside the village and knocked on the door. An amiable butler answered the door promptly, "How can I help you?"

"Is the Señor in need of a gardener?" José asked meekly. The butler smiled, instantly taking a liking to this handsome, polite newcomer.

"The Señora does the interviewing. I'll fetch her."

José peeked in at the elegant foyer, a long winding staircase ran under a curved window through which he could see seagulls diving into the sea. The lady of the house, wife of Emilio the Spanish banker, an angelic, porcelain skinned, green-eyed goddess, glided down into his view, filling José's heart with pure elation.

"Welcome, come in. You're looking for work as a gardener?"

José obediently took a step in, entranced by the Tuscan beauty. He stopped himself from falling to his knees by placing a hand on the side of the door for balance. The Señora rushed over to help him to a bench on the side of the foyer, sitting so close that her scent made him dizzy.

"You don't remember me?" he managed, staring longingly into her olive irises.

She shook her head, then turned a bright shade of pink, "Those days are long behind me, I was young and poor...it was a different time..."

"No, no, Noemi, it's me!"

She bounced up, alarmed. Nobody had called her that name in many years, an identity she left behind on purpose. She adored her tranquil life with Emilio, exploring the beaches on horseback and flying to Marseille for the high holidays. She pointed firmly towards the open door.

"Our garden is taken care of! Please, leave. Don't make me call my husband!"

"It's me, José! I've been searching for you for years!"

"Gino!"

Noemi scurried off up the staircase. The butler pushed a sobbing José out of the house, slamming and locking the door. José collapsed on the doorstep. He had expected her to recognize him, for them to elope in the night so they could live out the rest of their lives in some remote corner of the world. José had never considered that Noemi wouldn't remember one of the hundreds of clients she had serviced in Florence. He'd had years to inflate their non-existent relationship.

The ex-pilot trudged to the cliff's edge, peering through a deluge of tears down the rocky crags. Choppy waves foamed. From his pocket, he pulled out the time travel device.

He thumbed in the activation combination, entered in a number and a direction, and lifted his head towards the heavens. There was nothing left for him in this world.

Without a second thought, he threw himself off the cliff, accelerating straight at a sharp rock jutting from the seething water. At the last possible second, he pressed the screen of the time travel device. A flash of blue appeared, followed by a flash of green.

CPSIA information can be obtained
at www.ICGtesting.com
Printed in the USA
BVHW090036171221
624207BV00016B/839

9 780578 333267